DEADLY RAINS
A WITCH IN THE WOODS

JENNA ST. JAMES

Deadly Rains

Jenna St. James

Copyright © 2024 by Jenna St. James.

Published by Jenna St. James

All Rights Reserved. No part of this publication may be reproduced without the written permission of the author.

This is a work of fiction. Names and characters are either the product of the author's imagination or are used fictitiously, and any resemblance to actual persons, living or dead, business establishments, events, or locales is entirely coincidental.

❦ Created with Vellum

I

"*This rain is ridiculous, Princess,*" Needles grumbled from the backseat of my old, beat up Bronco.

I didn't argue with my talking and flying porcupine partner because he was correct. The rain was ridiculous. For the past week and a half, Enchanted Island had experienced daily torrential downpours. We usually have a rainy season, yes. After all, April showers bring May flowers…but this was so far past rainy season. We were now heading into monsoon territory.

Even my dad, Black Forest King, said he couldn't remember a time the island had sustained so much rain. And along with the rain…came environmental damage. Mostly just landslides and downed trees for right now.

Which was why I currently patrolled the backroads on the central part of the island—just south of the northern border—windshield wipers on high, and hands gripping the wheel. Every law enforcement person was on call—even the former sheriff, Walt Hawkins.

As the Game Warden for Enchanted Island, I wore many hats. As long as I have my monthly reports in on time, the mayor and island council pretty much let me make my own hours. Helping out the citizens and the island itself with daily patrolling while the rains came was a service I didn't mind performing.

The ringing of my cell phone had me pulling over to the side of the one-lane road. Turning on my emergency flashers, I slid my hand over the green icon on the screen as my friend's name popped up. I immediately put him on speakerphone so Needles could hear. "Hey, Tommy. What's up?"

"Got something for you, Shayla," he said.

Tommy Trollman was a childhood friend. I hadn't had many of those growing up. Outside of my cousin, Serena, who was ten years younger than me, I could count the number of friends I had on one hand—with three leftover fingers. When your dad is Black Forest King, most kids stay far away. But not Tommy. By the time he was in third grade, he was nearly six feet tall. One day, Mom and I traveled into town to do some shopping, and two older werewolf boys gave me chase. Mom was in the store, so I did the only thing I could do…I took off running. I could have just zapped them with magic and been done with it, but it just wasn't my way. When they were about to catch me, Tommy stepped out between two buildings and clotheslined the mean boys. He then picked them up by their shirts, rattled their bones, and threw them down the sidewalk.

We'd immediately bonded.

We had each other's backs during junior high and high school. He was also fiercely protective of Serena as well. Tommy was what my law-enforcement husband, Alex Stone, called a loan shark with a heart. Tommy owned Boos & Brews, a local watering hole in town popular with the supernaturals.

"Again?" I mused. "You turned me on to my last case as well." I chuckled and turned down my windshield wipers one notch. "You thinking of getting your PI license soon?"

His deep laugh filled the cab of my Bronco. "Not likely. And this isn't a rumor I've heard. This is me knee-deep in it, Shayla."

Something in Tommy's voice had me instantly on alert. I turned and faced Needles—our eyes both wide. "What's going on, Tommy?"

"You know where Across the Bridge Trinkets is?" he asked.

I frowned and searched frantically in my head. "I think so. Over by the old stone tower?" I smiled. "I haven't thought of that place in years—both the tower and the trinket store. I think the last time I was in there, I was with GiGi. I might have been seven or so. It's hard to spot, I remember that."

"Yep, you know the place I'm talking about."

"What aren't you telling me, Tommy?" I asked softly.

Tommy sighed. "I came out to Eldon Stonebridge's shop to talk business with him…and I found him, Shayla." He cleared his throat. "The old troll is dead. Murdered from the looks of it."

"Makes me mad when people kill on my island," Needles said, his wings glowing red and orange. *"Someone needs to pay!"*

"We'll be right there," I said to Tommy. "But why call me? Why not Alex?"

Tommy chuckled. "Two reasons. One, I knew it would rankle your husband, and I so love doing that."

"Right on!" Needles exclaimed.

"And the other reason is because I thought it might be your jurisdiction."

I frowned. "I don't know how."

"The moat and bridge, remember?" Tommy mused.

"That's right," I whispered. "I'd forgotten all about that."

In order to get to the store, the customer had to park and walk across a bridge that spanned a moat. There were two bridges if memory served—one to the parking lot, and the other straight out the back of the store which led to the forest.

"It might be a stretch," I said, "but I might be able to sell Alex on me having jurisdiction."

Tommy chuckled. "I have faith in you, Shayla."

"I'll call it in to Opal so she can send out Doc and Finn," I said, referring to our medical examiner and forensic scientist. "With this rain, I say give me ten minutes."

"I'll be here. Word to the wise, it's a treacherous drive out here on dry days. My truck made it just fine, and I suspect your Bronco will as well. But be careful. You remember how to get out here?"

"I have an interactive map on my phone of the entire island," I said. "I'll find it. And, Tommy, don't touch anything!"

"Wouldn't dream of it, PADA girl."

I grinned. "I'm no longer employed by PADA, Tommy. You know that."

Tommy snorted. "Once a PADA employee…always a PADA employee. See ya soon, Shayla."

We disconnected, and I couldn't help but think he was right in some ways. Having worked as a detective for the Paranormal Apprehension and Detention Agency until my retirement a few years back, I was still on call to help out when needed. When Alex and I had discovered a dead body on our honeymoon in the Bermuda Triangle, PADA had me take over the investigation. Of course, now they had a full-time PADA detective there, my friend Isla Ceartas, but before she'd arrived, the only law enforcement presence had been an elderly crab shifter sheriff.

Before pulling back onto the muddy dirt road, I called my

husband, Sheriff Alex Stone. He picked up on the second ring. "Wife, everything okay?"

I grinned. Even though we'd been married for a little over six months now, the endearment never got old.

"Needles and I are fine. You out patrolling?"

"On the west side of the island. What's up?"

"I just got a call from Tommy." Lightning splintered the sky, and four seconds later, booming thunder followed. "Anyway, he went out to Across the Bridge Trinkets to talk with the owner, Eldon Stonebridge. He said Mr. Stonebridge is dead."

"Why'd he call you and not dispatch?" Alex demanded.

I suppressed a smile. No way was I going to tell the truth and say because Tommy knew it would rankle Alex. "Because he thought it might be my jurisdiction."

"And why's that?"

I didn't need Alex sitting next to me to know he wasn't happy.

"Because the store is surrounded by water," I said.

Alex grunted. "How about I come out there too? We'll discuss jurisdiction."

"Of course," I said diplomatically…having no intention of backing down.

"We'll see, Gargoyle," Needles sneered from the back.

"I can hear you, Needles," Alex muttered.

Which was true. It hadn't always been that way, but now immediate family and friends could hear Needles talk thanks to my dad.

"I'll be out there as soon as I can," Alex said.

I disconnected, turned the windshield wipers back on high, and slowly made my way toward Across the Bridge Trinkets.

"What?" Needles mused. *"No lecture on playing nice with the gargoyle?"*

"Wouldn't do me any good."

I heard Needles chuckle. I'd have given him a glare in the rearview mirror, but I didn't want to take my eyes off the road. Mudslides were becoming more commonplace as the rain continued, and I didn't want to take the chance of damaging the Bronco…again.

2

"I figured I'd just wait outside in the parking lot for you," Tommy said as I stepped out of my Bronco and hurried over to where he stood, Needles hovering near my shoulder. "Before we go inside, I hope it's okay, but I put an extra jacket I had in my Jeep over a set of tire tracks. I didn't want the rain to wash any traces away." He shrugged and gave me a sheepish smile. "Could be I've watched too many supernatural crime dramas, but maybe you can get tire treads from it?"

"That's great, Tommy. Thanks." Calling the area a parking lot was generous. It was more a cleared area in the woods covered in mud and dirt and forest floor debris.

I strolled over to where the wet coat lay on the ground, waterlogged. Whispering under my breath, I erected a magical shield over the coat. It could be the tire tread had nothing to do with the murder, but it was better to be safe than sorry. "Why have a store out here?" I glanced around at the tall redwoods, sequoias, and pines, and then laughed. "Okay, I know why. It's absolutely beautiful, but he can't get much foot traffic out here. We are so far off the beaten path, it's not even funny."

"He doesn't get much business at all these days," Tommy said. "Which is why I'm here."

"Silent partner?" I mused, watching a trail of raindrops race down Tommy's black raincoat.

Tommy gave me a wolfish grin. "Something like that." The grin quickly faded, and sadness replaced the humor. "The old troll invited me out two months ago and laid it out for me."

I nodded. "I figured there had to be more to the story. This isn't your usual business venture."

"No. But Eldon knew my granddad, and so I felt I should do the right thing. Plus, he was coming to terms with the fact he only had one legal next-of-kin, and he was hesitant to leave her the store." He shrugged his massive shoulders. "So I bailed him out." He turned back and looked at the stone building. "I'm so mad, Shayla. This was totally unnecessary. Eldon had Swamp Whisper Syndrome. A condition only trolls get that leads to respiratory failure. There's no cure. He didn't have but maybe six months to live."

Tears filled my eyes. "Oh, Tommy. I'm so sorry." I laid my hand on his massive arm. "Before we go in, tell me about the layout. How many different ways in, do you know?"

"There's only this one-lane road. If you take it out past the store here, it will eventually dead end. It curves around like a backward 'c' so that the last house on the lane sits directly behind the store about a half-mile back and surrounded by trees. There are maybe four houses total on the road. As far as non-road entrances, once you cross the bridge in the back of the store, Eldon's house is the first cottage just off the beaten path in the forest. You can actually see his roof from the back of the store. Then, if you follow the stone path even farther into the woods, there's that house I mentioned that is on this dead-end road. The entire forested area is owned by Eldon. So he had the store, his cottage, thirty acres of forest, and the house that sits at the dead end directly behind the store."

I conjured up a pair of regular-sized booties and gloves for me and troll-sized booties and gloves for Tommy. "I don't want to contaminate the scene any more than I'm sure it is."

Tommy nodded and donned the items. "I didn't see mud or anything when I entered the store, just the physical mess. It wasn't until I walked behind the counter that I found Eldon on the floor." He winced. "I'm really sorry about messing up your crime scene."

I waved his concern away. "You couldn't have known." I gave him an appraising look. "Why were you here, Tommy?"

Tommy sighed. "Honestly? Just to check on the old guy. We'd already signed our papers a while back, and everything is mine. I promised him I wouldn't take over though until he passed away. He said the only thing he asked was that I come out and see him once a week. I figured he was just lonely and wanted to talk." He shrugged. "It's not like I have much to do, so I was more than happy to drive out here."

"It's a beautiful area of the island."

Tommy motioned for me to go first over the narrow, moss-covered stone bridge. Pushing back the hood on my raincoat, Needles settled on my shoulder.

"Why a moat?" I asked.

Tommy chuckled. "Added to the charm, according to Eldon. He built it when he built the store some fifty-plus years ago. He said it was funny because it was true. Trolls love their bridges and moats."

I stepped off the bridge and made a right, stepping onto the cobblestone steps. The store hadn't changed much in the thirty-something years I'd last seen it. Made of stone and wood, the small building surrounded by a moat and bridge seemed a natural part of the forest setting.

"I left the door open because it was already open," Tommy said. "I worried about that until I realized the overhang would keep out most of the driving rain."

I nodded. "Yeah, there shouldn't—"

I broke off when I felt an all-too-familiar pull in my belly. Needles sensed it too because he sprang from my shoulder, his wings glowing red and blue.

"I feel it too, Needles," I said.

"Feel what?" Tommy asked.

"The trees are...upset."

One of the traits I'd inherited from my dad was the ability to communicate with plants and animals. Sometimes it was just a feeling being conveyed, while other times it was an actual verbal conversation.

"Hurry, Princess," Needles said, zipping ahead of me. *"We need to find out what's wrong!"*

"Stay here," I said to Tommy before sprinting around the building to the back of the store. Once there, I had to cross another moss-covered stone bridge that spanned the moat. Cocking my head, I listened to where the lamenting was coming from.

"This way!"

I followed Needles and barely glanced at what I assumed was Eldon's cottage as I jogged down the path. I was having a hard time running in the booties. Without missing a beat, I stopped, yanked them off my black work boots, and shoved them in my uniform pocket. The last thing I needed to do was fall and break something.

When Needles came to an abrupt stop, I realized we'd gotten

off the rocky path and were now standing under a canopy of trees so thick, I no longer felt the rain.

"We did what we could to hide them," a timid rabbit said as she hopped out from behind a tree. "We even tried hiding their footprints with our tracks."

I glanced down and smiled. "Smart thinking. Thank you for keeping them safe. What is your name?"

"I'm Brixlee, and I live in that underground hole over there."

I glanced over to where she pointed. "Where are they?"

I still had no idea what was going on.

A bushy-tailed squirrel ran down the trunk of a nearby tree. "I'm Vip. And they're hiding in that fallen log over there."

3

"Everything okay, Shayla?"

I turned and rolled my eyes. "I told you to stay put, Tommy."

The giant troll grinned. "Sure. I'm going to hide away while you take off running toward danger? Not a chance. I'd run after you even *without* the threat of your husband kicking my butt if I let something happen to you."

Needles snickered. *"Now that's a fight I'd like to see."*

"What's going on?" Tommy mused.

I put a finger to my lips, and then pointed to the hollowed-out fallen log a short distance away.

Narrowing his eyes, Tommy stalked toward the log. Lifting my hands in a mock strangle pose, I followed silently after the big guy. Short of using magic to keep him immobile, I was just going to have to accept his help.

"Come out," Tommy ordered in a voice even deeper and more menacing than his naturally deep voice. When no one emerged, Tommy crossed his arms over his chest and scowled. "If I have to upend this log, I will. Can't weight much."

I snickered. "Just four hundred pounds." I lifted my hands, readying my magic. I had no idea what or who was inside.

"They're scared," Needles said.

I nodded. "I can hear the trees making soothing sounds. I assume whoever it is won't be a threat." I lowered my hands and tiptoed past Tommy. "Hello. My name is Agent Loci-Stone. I'm the game warden for Enchanted Island. I need you to come out, please."

After a few seconds, I heard the faint sounds of rustling inside the log. A few seconds later, the large pile of banana leaves that had been covering the entrance to the log fell away, and a little boy of about five or six crawled out.

"Hello," he whispered to the ground.

"Are you—"

I broke off when a woman poked her head out. "My daughter's also with me. Please, don't hurt us."

"Of course we won't," Tommy said, leaning down to help the woman out.

Whimpering, the woman's eyes went wide, and she instinctively hunched her shoulders and scrambled backward inside the log. "Jacob! Hurry! Get back insi—"

"I'm not going to hurt you," Tommy soothed. "I'm friends with Agent Loci-Stone."

I could hear the poor woman panting in fear, and my heart broke. "Ma'am." I squatted down and looked inside the log. "No one is going to hurt you."

Eyes closed and nodding, the woman drew in a couple deep breaths. "Of course. I'm sorry. I just got frightened."

"Understandable." I reached down and extended my hand, hoping to help her exit the log. "What's your name?"

"Pepper," she squeaked.

"Let me grab your daughter." I reached for the little girl who looked to be in the toddler stage, then stopped short when Pepper gasped and put a protective hand over the girl's head. "Never mind. I'll just step back so you can crawl out on your own."

The little boy, with his wide, fearful eyes, was staring up at Tommy, his mouth agape. The sight of his small body trembling in fear was a kick to the gut. I knew if I was feeling it…Tommy was also feeling it. Not every troll was large. It just so happened Tommy was.

"I'm sorry for overreacting," Pepper said once she was out of the log and staggering to her feet. "We just weren't—" When she caught sight of Tommy, she broke off and mimicked her young son…wide eyed and trembling.

"You're like a mountain," Jacob whispered.

Tommy smiled. "I guess I am."

"Up! Up!" the little girl cried, reaching up with arms outstretched and fists clenching and unclenching. "Up! Momma!"

Tommy chuckled. "She's adorable."

And she really was…cheeks all pink and rosy, expressive blue eyes, curly blonde hair that was still baby fine. When it became apparent she wasn't going to be lifted into Tommy's arms, she started to squirm. "Down!"

"Mia, no," Pepper snapped.

The little girl slowly turned in her mother's arms. The incredulous look on Mia's face was so comical, if the situation wasn't so serious, I'd have laughed. The little spitfire reminded me of Jayden, Zac Spark's little girl. If I had to guess, I'd say Jayden was just a little older than Mia, but not by much.

"She's a sassy little one, isn't she?" Needles landed on my shoulder, his wings glowing purple and green.

Mia squealed and clapped her hands when she saw Needles. "Want! Want!"

Once again, her tiny little fists clenched and unclenched.

"I'm a one-woman porcupine," Needles joked. *"Already got me a girl. Sorry, love."*

Mia babbled and laughed, bucking against her mom.

Jacob still hadn't said a word…not even when he saw Needles. He was now firmly attached to his mom's leg, eyes wide, not speaking.

"Have you seen Mr. Stonebridge?" Pepper asked, tears filling her blue eyes. "Do you know he's…" She glanced at her son, not finishing the sentence.

"Mr. Stonebridge is hurt," Jacob said. "He was on the floor, and he wasn't moving. I saw blood." His lower lip trembled. "I don't think he's going to get up."

I glanced up at Tommy, and he gave me a small nod. "My husband, Sheriff Alex Stone, should be along shortly. Until then, I'd like you to stay here with Tommy." I placed my hand on Tommy's arm. "Tommy Trollman is a dear friend, and you can trust him."

"Oh," Pepper whispered. "You're the man who was helping Eldon?"

"Yes," Tommy said. "You know about that?"

Pepper smiled. "Eldon and I used to talk a lot." She brushed a tear from her cheek. "He was such a kind man."

"I'll be back shortly," I said to Pepper and Tommy.

"Catch!" Mia screamed as she leaped out of her mom's arms and latched onto Tommy's chest…like she was part flying squirrel.

Laughing, Tommy pushed the little girl up his chest until she was sitting on one shoulder, looking around.

"It's okay," I heard him say as I turned to walk away. "I have tons of nieces and nephews, and they all think I'm a mountain that needs to be climbed."

4

The first thing I noticed when I stepped inside Across the Bridge Trinkets' back door was the elderly troll lying on the floor. The young boy was correct...blood was pooled near Eldon's head. The outside edges were already dark and crusted, making me believe he had been dead for at least an hour, even with the extra moisture and humidity in the air.

Conjuring up new gloves and booties, I quickly slipped them on.

"I don't like this part of the investigation," Needles said, his wings glowing the same crimson color as the blood on the floor. *"But I know it's necessary for me to be here now. Especially since I'll be working closely with Zoie, Brick, and Harlow. They will need me at all parts of the investigation. Even the examination."*

It was true. Needles could probably skip the autopsy results as long as Harlow filled him in, but for everything else, Needles would be an integral part of their working dynamic.

"I don't see a murder weapon." I stood and glanced around

the room, giving it my full attention for the first time. "What a mess."

Mess was putting it mildly. Nearly every shelf had been tipped over, trinkets and baubles broken and scattered across the floor.

"Yeah, someone was pissed," Needles agreed.

I walked over to the edge of the counter and noticed a broken jar of what looked like blackberry jam. The glass shards and jelly were on the floor, but on the counter was the label. Leaning down, I read the words, and my heart dropped to my stomach. *Blackberry Jam. Made by Pepper Hollis.*

Did this mean the killer knew Pepper had discovered the body? What kind of danger would this put her and her children in? How had the killer known Pepper was in the store? All questions I needed to ask Pepper when I interviewed her.

"It looks like someone tried to break into the cabinet here," Needles said, hovering in front of a large curio cabinet.

I placed my gloved hand on the cabinet and nodded. "There's powerful magic here. Eldon definitely wanted something kept in."

I scanned the shelves behind the sealed glass and frowned. "It just looks like vintage toys. Action figures, mostly. Could they have really been that expensive?"

"Action figures and other collectibles can be extremely valuable," my husband said as he stepped inside the front door of Across the Bridge Trinkets.

Rain was dripping off his head and clothes and pooling around his boots. Even drenched, he looked sexy as hell in his sheriff's uniform.

"Oh, is it still raining outside?" I teased.

His stoic, handsome face split into a grin. "Sprinkling."

I conjured up another pair of gloves and booties and walked

across the floor, careful not to step on any of the broken glass, and handed him the items.

"This is our jurisdiction, Gargoyle," Needles said. *"He's surrounded by a body of water."*

"Man-made body of water," Alex grumbled. "And it's a moat."

"We can argue over who will take the lead later," I said. "Right now, we have bigger fish to fry. Not only do we have a dead body, but we have a witness and two children." I pointed to the label on the counter. "And our killer may know who they are."

"Walk me through it, Shayla," Alex said.

So I did. I told him what Needles and I experienced when we got out of the Bronco, how we found Pepper and her children hiding in a log, and how they were all now with Tommy.

Alex's lips twitched. "If this wasn't so serious, I might enjoy the thought of the towering troll being taken down a peg or two by a two-year-old."

We walked over to where Eldon lay on the floor.

"I know Doc will have to sign off," I said, "but it looks like blunt force trauma to the head. No sign of a murder weapon right now. But then again, the store is an absolute mess. Hard to say what could've been used to kill him."

I heard a car pull up outside and figured that was Doc and Finn.

"I have Grant patrolling the south and east sides of the island," Alex said. "In the last three hours, he's had two calls about landslides and a roof leak." He glanced outside as thunder rumbled, shaking the windows of the small store. "And it doesn't look like the storm is gonna let up anytime soon. Normally, Shayla, I would fight you on this one for jurisdictional lead, but I can't. Grant, Deputy Sparks, and even Walt are stepping up to help me patrol the island. Grant and I will be here for anything you need, background, whatever. But I have no problem with you assuming lead on this one."

Doc and Finn stepped through the front door, both of them releasing their umbrellas. With a wave of her hand, Finn used her magic to turn the umbrellas upside down and hover them outside under the overhang. Doc handed her a set of booties and gloves, and the two of them donned their protective gear before striding over to where we stood near Eldon's body.

"Oh, Eldon," Doc murmured. "I'm sorry, friend."

I blinked in surprise. "I guess I shouldn't be surprised you knew him. I'm sorry for your loss."

Doc nodded, pressing his lips together as he squatted down next to Eldon's body. "Thank you, Shayla. Cursory examination shows a gash on his head. Blood on the ground. Looks like blunt force trauma."

When he reached in to grab a thermometer from his doctor bag, I glanced away. "There's a label on the counter here. It has the witness' name on it. I believe our killer knows Pepper Hollis was in the store."

"Why do you say that?" Alex asked.

"Because no way does this jar of jam get dropped, and Pepper has the presence of mind to pick it up and put it on the counter before fleeing. No, I don't see that happening. I haven't spoken with her yet. I was waiting for you."

"You think she's in danger?" Alex asked.

"Don't see how she couldn't be." I stepped aside so Finn could put the label in an evidence bag.

"Eldon Stonebridge and Barton Longtree were lifelong rivals," Doc said without looking up. "I'm not saying Barton did this. I don't believe he did. But I think you should know about the conflict."

"Why were they enemies?" Alex asked.

"That's for Barton to say." Doc sighed, stood, and glanced outside the open door where the rain was still coming down. "Suffice it to say, there was more than one reason."

I nodded. "Thanks, Doc. I'll be sure to question Barton Longtree."

"What do you say we go question Pepper?" Alex mused.

Before I could answer, his phone went off. "It's Opal." He slid his finger across the icon. "This is Sheriff Stone, Opal. What do you got for me?"

Whatever Opal was saying, Alex wasn't happy. He did a lot of nodding and grunting, but no actual words.

"Got it. I'll take care of it now. Thanks, Opal." Sighing, he disconnected and shoved the phone in his pocket. "Going to have to take a rain check on the interview." He flashed me a grin. "A little pun for you, wife. Anyway, we have two separate calls about stalled vehicles and water on the road. Weston and his tow truck can't get there for another hour, so I want to go check on them real quick. Make sure everyone is safe." He leaned over and kissed my cheek. "When you have a list of suspects, text them to me, and I'll make sure Grant and I get right on it. Be careful. See you tonight."

5

Slipping off my booties and gloves once again, Needles and I hurried across the bridge, past Eldon's cottage, and stepped off the path to hurry through the forest.

It didn't take long to find Tommy and the others. Mainly, I followed the giggles and voices. I was glad the forest once again had a sense of peace and calmness washing over it. The plants, trees, and animals seemed appeased, no longer anxious.

Pepper Hollis was sitting on a log, watching her two children chase Tommy. The small smile hovering on her lips seemed a little too sad for me. There was a lot about this woman that seemed too sad for me.

"I'll go play with the children, Princess," Needles said.

Evidently, Needles felt the woman's sorrow as well.

"Thank you," I whispered.

Plastering a smile on my face, I strolled over to where the haggard young woman sat and motioned to the empty spot next to her. "Do you mind if I sit?"

She shook her head. "Of course not."

Eyes still on her children, I took a minute to study her. She wasn't just petite…she was tiny. She looked like she could blow away with one big gust of wind. Her hair was limp and thin, and there were dark circles under her eyes. She had the look of a woman not getting enough food or sleep.

"I've been sitting here terrified," she whispered. "I'm scared of what this may do to my children. They liked Eldon, and now he's dead. They saw that. How do they come back from that?"

"I honestly don't know," I said. "They look like they're handling things quite well, but if you're still nervous, I can give you the name of a psychologist on the island."

Pepper snorted and turned hard eyes on me. "I can't afford therapy. I don't even have a car."

"Childhood trauma is not something we take lightly on the island," I said. "Our psychologist offers counseling for free to children under eighteen, and he's paid quite well by the island council to offer that service."

Pepper frowned. "I've never heard of such a thing."

"We do a lot of things differently on Enchanted Island. How long have you been here?"

"Just a little over a year." She tucked a piece of stray hair behind her ears. "I knew no one when I moved here. I was sitting with my children at the Enchanted Island Cafe when I noticed someone selling jams near the register. I asked the lady working if she was looking for more product, but she said no. Then she gave me Eldon's name."

I grinned. "You probably spoke to Danica Spriteson. I went to school with her. I think she lived out this way, if memory serves correctly."

Pepper nodded. "That's what she said. She asked me if I was new in town, and I said yes. She asked me if my children and I had a safe place to stay, and she must've seen something on my face because she patted my hand and said she knew someone who could help me." Pepper wiped a tear from her eye. "She gave me Eldon's name, then when her shift ended, she drove me out here. I told Eldon I could make jams and weave baskets." She gave a small laugh…which ended on a sob. "He looked around his tinker shop and said, 'That's just the sort of thing we need here.' Can you believe that? He sells wind chimes and garden ornaments and other home knickknacks, but not jams and baskets. He didn't really need my things." Tears filled her eyes and slowly ran down her cheeks. "And then he said he had a tiny cottage, not much, but probably big enough for me and my children if we wanted to stay there. No charge, he said." She snorted. "Told me I'd be doing him a favor because it just sits empty." She blew out a breath and looked away. "That's when Danica left. She hugged me and said I'd be in good hands. And I was. Do you know Eldon even let me come in on Sunday nights and clean the store for extra income?"

"What all did you do?"

"I dusted and swept, mostly. You know, just make sure the place looked good for the coming week."

Nodding, I glanced over at the kids. "Why isn't your son in school today? I assume he's old enough to attend?"

Pepper glanced at her son. "He is. I've just elected to homeschool him."

"So you and Eldon were close?" I asked.

"I guess you could say that. He was real good to me and my kids. And he didn't have to be. He didn't know me at all."

"When was the last time you spoke with him?"

"I think two days ago? He didn't know we were coming by today. We wanted to surprise him. I told him the blackberries were almost ready to be picked, and that when I had the jelly ready, I'd stop by with new jams and jellies. The store doesn't open until 10:00 on weekdays, so I thought we'd just slip in right before the store opened and people arrived."

I nodded. "Okay. Do you think you can tell me what happened? What did you see?"

Pepper ran her hands over her face. "I should've paid more attention. But Jacob was all excited and chattering, and, well, as you can see, Mia is just a handful." She gave a small laugh. "So, anyway, we had walked across the bridge like usual." She looked up at me. "We always enter the back way. That was something Eldon allowed me to do. Sometimes, if there were people inside, he'd come out and meet me outside to get my things or to pay me. He was thoughtful that way."

It was obvious either Pepper Hollis didn't want to be seen by locals, or she didn't like being around people in general.

"I stepped inside, and at first I didn't see him. I was more shocked at the chaos. All the shelves had been overturned, and everything looked broken. I set the basket on the edge of the counter, and I think I turned, and that's when I saw Eldon on the floor." She wrapped her arms around her waist and leaned forward. "It just makes me sick thinking about not only Eldon being killed, but how close I came to letting my children get hurt."

"Can you explain?"

Pepper sat up straighter. "When I saw Eldon, I was so shocked that I instinctively backed up and hit the basket of jams I had placed on the counter. I didn't even have time to think about using my magic to stop the basket from dropping. I was just so shocked. The basket fell, and the jams scattered, breaking on the ground." Her eyes locked on mine, and if it was possible, her skin lost even more of its color. "That's when I heard the car door slam outside. Maybe they said something? I don't know. I really don't. I just grabbed my kids, and we ran out the back. I don't even remember crossing the bridge. I just remember I was panting and carrying Mia and yelling at Jacob to run." Pepper leaned over, resting her head on her knees. When her teeth finally stopped chattering, she sat back up. "I looked back when we got off the path, and I could see someone inside the store, like their silhouette. I think they were wearing a raincoat, so I don't know if it was a man or a woman. I just knew we had to hide. I saw the log, and I told Jacob to get in, and then I went in behind him with Mia still in my arms. I used my magic and gathered a ton of leaves near the entrance and performed a cloaking spell so we couldn't be detected."

"That was smart thinking."

Pepper gave a shaky laugh. "I don't know how I thought of it. So many things were screaming in my head. Anyway, I was whispering to the kids that they had to be quiet, and that we couldn't be found."

I placed my hand on her arm, mainly because she had gone deathly white and her teeth were chattering. "It's good they understood your urgency to be quiet."

Pepper closed her eyes, tears streaming down her face. "I wouldn't exactly say it's a good thing my kids know how to hide and be quiet and not draw attention to themselves."

"You are running from someone." I didn't say it like a question. I knew she was running.

"Yes," she whispered.

"What happened next?" I asked.

"I heard someone walking in the forest. I could hear the sound of them moving, even though it's pretty wet out here. I know they passed by the log, but then they walked away."

"How long do you think you were in the log before we found you?"

Pepper shrugged and shook her head. "I don't know. Five

minutes? Thirty minutes? When you're afraid for your life, time sort of stands still and fast forwards all at the same time."

I smiled. "I understand. Do you know of anyone who would want to hurt Eldon?"

Again, Pepper shrugged and shook her head. "Not really. I mean, not enough that they would kill him."

"Any name you could give me is helpful."

Pepper sighed. "A couple months ago, me and the kids came to drop off some jams, and I heard some arguing in the store." She slid her eyes to me. "I notice those things. Angry voices. Anyway, I had the kids stay on the bridge while I went inside the store. Eldon was arguing with this man. They didn't see me, and afterward, when the man left, I asked Eldon who he was. Eldon said his name was Dalton Fowler, and he makes the wind chimes and lawn ornaments for the store."

"Do you know what they were arguing about?"

Pepper nodded. "Sort of. I think it had to do with the percentage Eldon takes from the profits. I think Eldon was going to take more from Mr. Fowler. But I'm not exactly sure. It was pretty heated, though. Eldon told Dalton if he didn't like the change, then he could just sell his stuff to Barton Longtree in town at Fairy Lights. Eldon then told Dalton he knew about him and Ellie." She shrugged. "I don't know who Ellie is, but Dalton seemed shocked."

"What did Dalton do?"

"He got mad and stormed out the front door."

A piercing scream lit up the forest, and Pepper and I both turned just in time to see Mia levitating herself just out of Tommy's reach. I could tell Tommy was nervous, but he was trying to act nonchalant and cool as he tried to snatch Mia out of the air. Needles was hovering near a worried Jacob—shaking his head and smiling, his wings glowing green and purple.

"Mia," Tommy called softly. "I need you to come down now. You're starting to scare me."

Mia laughed again and moved just out of Tommy's reach. Waving her hand, the little minx made one of the large banana leaves high in the treetop tip over, dumping rainwater on top of Tommy's head.

Pepper jumped to her feet, her mouth open in a silent scream. She stumbled, then looked up, gasping for air. "Mia, no!" Her eyes flew to Tommy. "She didn't mean it. Please don't—"

Tommy threw back his head and laughed, deep and loud. He laughed so hard his shoulders shook, and he had to grab his side as he bent over, wheezing, trying to catch his breath. Even Jacob, who'd been just as horrified as his mother, relaxed enough to watch Tommy laugh and smiled as well.

That alone was enough to shatter my heart. This family had gone through some serious trauma. And it went far beyond seeing Eldon Stonebridge dead on the floor.

"Oh, you're a cheeky little one, Miss Mia," Tommy said.

"He's not mad?" Pepper mused.

I snorted. "No, Tommy's not mad. It would take more than a little girl dumping water on his head to make Tommy mad." I patted the log. "Come sit. It's okay. I'm almost done with the questions."

Pepper looked once more at her children before turning back to me and sitting down on the log.

"Do you know what time you got here today?" I asked.

"We left our cottage around 9:30. We always walk through the forest since our cottage is directly behind the store. Otherwise, we'd have to walk the road, and I don't want that. It doesn't take more than twenty or thirty minutes to walk here with the kids, depending on if we stop and do some exploring. With the rain coming down, I didn't let the kids linger. So we were definitely here before 10:00, before the store officially opened. Maybe 9:45 or so?"

I caught Tommy's eyes and motioned him over with my head. I figured I could ask Tommy what time he arrived so I could get a better understanding of when Eldon's death may have occurred. If Pepper heard someone outside just minutes after coming through the back door, then she had to have just missed the killer.

Pepper dropped her head into her hands. "I know this sounds horrible to even say, but what now? Eldon owned that cottage. Do we have to move? Do you think his niece will inherit? I'm not sure where me and my kids will go. I've been here a year, but I pretty much keep to myself. I'm sorry to say Eldon was pretty much my only friend."

"I may be able to help with that," Tommy said.

Pepper and I both glanced up. Tommy was hovering nearby, hands in his pockets. The kids were busy chasing Needles and a couple other woodland creatures around.

My eyes widened. "Your agreement included the extra cottage as well?" I couldn't keep the surprise out of my voice. "Why would he do that?"

Tommy's lips twisted into an almost smile. "Oh, I think Eldon Stonebridge was sneakier than even I gave him credit for." His eyes slid to Pepper. "I am your new landlord, not Eldon's niece."

6

"Oh." Pepper looked up at Tommy and gave him a hesitant smile, her neck and cheeks pink.

I stood and brushed the wood chips and mud off my pants. "Pepper, I'd like you to stick around, please. I need to speak to Tommy real quick, but I won't be long."

Pepper looked up through the thick canopy of trees and smiled. "Looks like the rain has lightened up a little. That's a nice reprieve. I'll just go help my kids blow off some energy."

She made a wide berth around Tommy and hurried over to where Needles, Jacob, and Mia were playing.

"So," I said, "Eldon signed over his store, his cottage, his acreage, and his rental cottage all to you?"

Tommy scowled. "I know how it looks. I told him when I signed the agreement that I wasn't happy. I didn't want all of it. I actually just wanted to help the old troll out, but he wouldn't take a loan. He insisted I buy it all." He looked over his shoulder and smiled. "I think now I understand why. He probably knew if his niece inherited, she'd just kick Pepper out."

I arched an eyebrow. "And you won't?"

He and I both knew he would never kick out Pepper and her two children.

Tommy ran his hand across the back of his neck. "No, I won't be kicking her out."

"Okay, let's talk about Eldon. When was the last time you spoke to him?"

"This morning around 9:30. I told him I was leaving my house and needed to run an errand real quick, and then I'd be there. I probably got to Across the Bridge Trinkets just a little after 10:00. I remember thinking the store would have just opened when I parked in the parking lot."

"So if Pepper and the kids got here around 9:45, then they probably hid in the log for about twenty minutes."

Tommy winced. "I can't imagine the fear they must have experienced."

"I know Pepper came through the back," I said. "What about you? I think you said you came in through the front?"

Tommy nodded. "Yes. It was open, so I just came in. Of course, the first thing I noticed was all the broken merchandise on the floor. I thought there had been a robbery, and so, of course, I went immediately looking for Eldon. It didn't take me long to find him behind the counter."

"In your dealings with Eldon, did he ever mention having a problem with anyone? Did he seem scared? Or maybe he mentioned someone angry at him?"

"I know he and Barton Longtree have been rivals for many years." Tommy smiled. "But, then again, a lot of us are rivals with Barton. He's a crotchety old fairy. Eldon never married, never had kids. I'm afraid I can't give you much insight into his personal life other than he didn't care for his niece and her son."

"His niece? So that means Eldon either has a brother or a sister?"

Tommy nodded. "He had an older brother, but he passed away about two years ago."

A high-pitched squeal pierced the air, and Tommy and I both turned to look. Once again, Mia was levitated in the air, arms outstretched. "Tommy! Play!"

Tommy chuckled. "She's adorable, but her mom is going to have her hands full." Tommy took two steps toward the girl. "You be careful, Miss Mia."

That just seemed to make the little girl laugh even more. Needles zipped over to where she hovered, his wings glowing purple and green.

Pepper strolled toward us, her son still attached to her side. "I don't know why Mia is doing this. Showing off like she is. Usually, she doesn't take to men." She put her hand on her son's head and smoothed back his hair. "My daughter..."

"Is awesome!" Needles shouted, doing a somersault in the air.

Mia squealed and also turned a somersault in the air.

There was something about the way the little girl was staring at Needles. Like she understood what he was saying. I narrowed my eyes at her, then turned to Needles. "Can she understand you, Needles?"

"Funny! Hello, birdie!" Mia held out her hand and tried to pet Needles on the head.

"Bird! Do I look like a bird? If I wasn't so taken with the little beast, I'd—"

"Do you think the bad man will come for us?" Jacob whispered, cutting off Needles' unheard tirade.

"No." Tommy knelt until he was level with the scared boy. "I promise you, Jacob. I won't let anything happen to you or your sister or your mother."

"Promise?" Jacob whispered.

Tommy held out his huge hand to the boy. "Promise." When Jacob finally put his small hand in Tommy's for a handshake, Tommy stood and looked at Pepper. "You don't have to worry about leaving the cottage or for your safety. Even if I have to camp out in your front yard to keep you safe the next few days until Shayla apprehends the killer, I will do that."

Pepper's face turned bright red. "Oh, I don't think you'll have to sleep in the front yard. Besides, I'm sure you have better things to do."

Tommy laughed. "I actually don't."

"You don't have a job that would miss you?" she asked.

Tommy waved his hand dismissively in the air. "I own a lot of property on the island, and I own a bar in town. I have plenty of employees who can run my business."

My cell phone dinged, and I pulled it out of my pocket. It was from Finn. "Looks like we have company. A man and a woman. They're not pleased with the barrier Finn erected in front of the door. They are demanding to speak to the person in charge. They are heading to Eldon's cottage." I sighed. "Needles, if it's the niece and her son, I need Tommy with me to go over the agreement. I can't imagine this is going to go over well. I don't want to leave Pepper and her kids here alone. Do you mind staying?"

Needles' wings glowed gold, and he gave me a snappy salute. "I will protect them with my life, Princess."

Because I knew Needles was serious, I turned to Pepper. "I don't have time to explain. Just know when I say Needles will protect you with his life, it's an absolute truth."

7

"Have you met the niece and her son?" I asked as Tommy and I strode through the forest toward Eldon's cottage.

"I have not."

"Obviously, you have a copy of the paperwork Eldon signed, but do you know if Eldon had a copy he kept in his cottage? I assume you don't have yours on you, and this could get ugly."

"I'm not sure where he kept it in his house. But I can have mine here in just a few minutes. I have a staff member who knows the combo to my safe. He can run it out to me."

I nodded. "Okay, if it comes to that, we'll do it. It shouldn't, though. Everything will be locked down. No one's getting in Eldon's house or the store until I say otherwise."

A couple stepped off the bridge and made a beeline for Eldon's stone cottage. Increasing our speed, Tommy and I jogged to cut them off.

"Excuse me," I said. "I'm going to need you to stop right there. I'm Agent Loci-Stone, the investigator in charge, and this property is off-limits right now."

The woman stopped, crossed her arms over her chest, and glared at me. "My uncle owns the shop and this home. What's going on? He told me to come out here today so we could talk, and now there are police everywhere. I demand to know what's going on?"

"Yeah," the younger man dressed in an oversized hoodie said. "What's going on?"

"Can you give me your names, please?" I asked.

"I am Gloria Stonebridge, and this is my son, Parker Stonebridge."

"Street name Stone." He pointed to the zipper pull on his hoodie where a turquoise stone sat at the base. "My invention. My brand. They're inner changeable too. Change your stone with your mood or outfit color." He winked at me. "You want one? Just hit me up. Got cute little girlie colors for the ladies."

"Parker's quite the entrepreneur," Gloria beamed. "I'm very proud of him. Pretty soon, he'll have his zipper pulls in all the clothing and collectible shops on the island."

"Stone, Ma!" Parker whined. "You gotta start calling me Stone."

I placed Gloria in maybe her mid-forties. She was a troll, so she wouldn't have magic for glamour to hide her true age, unless her son was doing that for her. Stone was half troll, half fairy.

"Yes, quite the entrepreneur," I murmured. "I assume you're Eldon's niece?"

Gloria raised an impatient hand in the air. "Obviously."

"I'm afraid I have some rather upsetting news," I said. "Eldon Stonebridge is dead."

Something flashed in her eyes. I couldn't tell if it was surprise, glee, or what it was...it was gone too fast.

"I'm sorry to hear that," she said. "He must've known he didn't have much time left and was calling me out here to let me know." She placed one hand on her chest and the other hand on her son's arm. "He probably wanted to let me know about his will. As his only heir, I'm sure he wanted me to have the store and his home."

"Don't forget the other cottage he had," Parker added quickly. "That will go to us as well."

Gloria nodded. "My son is correct. Eldon had two dwellings and his store." She shrugged and looked around. "I suppose all I need to do is figure out who his lawyer is, and we can wrap this unpleasantness up rather quickly. Do you know when we'll be able to get inside the house?"

"Never," Tommy said.

Gloria narrowed her eyes and stared up at Tommy. "Excuse me? Who are you?"

Tommy grinned. Having known Tommy most of my life, I knew this was not a grin his enemies ever wanted to see. This was an I-can-gobble-you-down-in-one-gulp grin. "I am the troll Eldon sold his store and two dwellings to."

"That's a lie!" Gloria exclaimed.

"You're a liar!" Parker echoed.

Tommy shrugged. "Believe it or don't, I don't care. I have the paperwork that says what our agreement was. Your uncle needed money, and so he came to me and offered to sell me his property. All of his property. Even the land."

"He should've told me he needed money!" Gloria cried. "Why didn't he tell me?"

"Why didn't he sell off those stupid toys he has?" Parker demanded. "Those collectibles would have held him over. I mean, we all know he didn't have that much longer to live."

"What collectibles?" I asked, knowing full well which ones they were probably talking about.

Gloria gasped. "Did someone steal his collection of action

figures and toys? Is that why he was killed? I thought it looked like someone had tossed his store when I glanced inside."

Parker nodded emphatically. "Yeah. They probably broke in, grabbed that metal fairy figurine he had on the counter, whacked him over the head, and stole everything. I bet the old troll didn't even have insurance on the collectibles or his store."

I held up my hand. "Can you describe this metal fairy figurine that was on his counter?"

Parker shrugged. "I dunno know. Just some metal statue of a fairy."

"Are you saying those action figures are gone?" Gloria asked. "Because if they are, then I demand the cops be called. He was robbed."

"Actually, he was murdered," I said.

Gloria threw up her hands. "Well, what are you waiting for? Get some real cops out here."

Tommy chuckled. "Yes, Agent Loci-Stone, get the real cops out here."

"I am the real cops, as you put it." I put quotes around the word real. "I am the person in charge of your uncle's murder investigation."

And the more they talked about this metal fairy statue, the more I was thinking that this could be the murder weapon.

"I just don't understand any of this," Gloria said. "Not only was he murdered, but now you're telling me that I'm not going to inherit? I want to speak to a lawyer."

I gave her a tight smile. "Gloria, I need to ask you and your son a few questions. When was the last time you both physically saw Eldon?"

"It's probably been about a month for me," Gloria said.

"Probably that long for me as well," Parker said.

I nodded. "When was the last time you spoke to him, Gloria?"

"He called me yesterday to say he wanted to see me around 11:30 today," Gloria said. "He wouldn't tell me what it was about, but I knew he was sick. I figured he wanted to talk about the store and what would happen once he was dead." She narrowed her eyes and glanced over at the store. "It never crossed my mind he would actually sell it without telling me."

"So you knew he was sick?" I asked.

"Yes, yes," Gloria said. "I've actually known for a while now. Like I said, I even came out here sometime last month to see if he needed help cataloging things. You know, for when he was gone? It would just make things simpler that way."

Tommy cursed under his breath.

"And you had no idea," I said slowly, watching her reaction, "that your uncle was probably going to tell you today that he had sold his business and both of his houses to someone else two months ago?"

Gloria pursed her lips. "I didn't kill my uncle, if that's what you're asking me."

I arched an eyebrow. "Okay. Where were the two of you this morning from 6:00 to 11:00?"

"I cannot speak for my son," Gloria said. "But I was at home. I woke up around 7:00, made some coffee and breakfast, and then took a shower and got ready. Stone arrived at my house around 11:00, and then we drove out here."

"And does anyone live with you?" I asked. "Anyone who could corroborate your statement?"

"I live alone."

I turned to Parker. "What about you? Where were you from 6:00 to 11:00?"

"Pretty much the same story," he said. "I woke up alone,

made some breakfast, hung around, then walked up to Mom's place."

"Walked?" I mused. "So you must live nearby?"

Parker shoved his hands in his front pockets. "Mom has a carriage house on her property. Well, technically, it was my granddad's property until he passed away. That's why Mom and I are here. I live in the carriage house, for privacy."

"Do you have a vehicle?" I asked Parker.

"Yeah, of course."

"Did you see your son's vehicle this morning?" I asked Gloria.

Gloria scoffed. "It's not like I can see his place from the main house. I have no idea if my son was home. But if he says he was, then I believe him."

I nodded. "Okay. Do you know of anyone who might have had it out for your uncle? Did he ever mention anyone being angry at him?"

"Not that I know of," Gloria said.

"You need to find that guy who wanted the collection," Parker said. "I've met him here before. Like a month or two ago, I heard him and Eldon yelling as I walked into the store."

"What guy?" I asked.

Parker shrugged. "His name is Linus. He's a witch. I know that much. He has long, dark hair to his shoulders. Pasty guy with these little round glasses. Looks like he never really leaves his home. I overheard him telling Uncle Eldon he needed to give his collection to a place that would respect it. Show it off, not hide it away. Uncle Eldon told him to go away and never come back."

I nodded. "Okay. I think that's all I have for now. Like I said, your uncle's property is off limits. And knowing Tommy is the new owner, I'm going to assume he does not want you on this property once I do release it."

Tommy folded his arms across his massive chest and glared down at Gloria and Parker. "You assume right, Agent Loci-Stone. And if I *do* see them around here, I will be calling the cops."

Gloria raised a finger in the air and stabbed it toward Tommy. "This isn't over!"

"Music to my ears," Tommy said. "Nothing I love more than a good fight."

8

I waited until Gloria and Parker stalked away before turning to Tommy. "Good luck with that. I don't see this going easy for you."

Tommy chuckled and dropped his hands to his sides. "Oh, I'm not worried about them. Everything Eldon and I agreed to is on the up and up. They have no legal leg to stand on if they try to contest it or sue me. I'm more worried about their alibi. There are a lot of holes there."

"I noticed."

"I'll tell you one thing, Shayla. It doesn't sit right with me having Pepper and her kids out here alone. I think Gloria and her son could make some trouble. I may not scare easily, but I can't say the same for that woman and her two kids. She looks scared of her shadow."

I arched an eyebrow. "What do you plan on doing?"

A slight blush ran up Tommy's neck, and the giant troll actually looked embarrassed as he shuffled his feet. "Maybe I really will camp out."

I snorted. "Let me know how that goes over."

Tommy grinned. "Yeah, it probably won't go over well."

"I'm gonna take a look around inside Eldon's house. Why don't you go relieve Needles and send him to me?"

"Can do."

Eldon's cottage was made from the same stone as the bridge and store. Two different types of ivy climbed the outside walls, and colorful wildflowers were just beginning to peek up from the dirt along the walkway and in the white window boxes. The wooden door, sage shutters, and thatched roof looked natural in the surrounding forest.

I wasn't the least bit surprised when I pushed open the front door. I hadn't expected Eldon to lock his place—after all, from his vantage point inside the store, he'd be able to see anyone walking toward his home.

"Wait for me, Princess."

Needles zipped over to me, his wings throwing off myriad colors. He usually got like that when he was excited or anxious. Seeing as how he'd just spent the last thirty minutes with two kids, I wasn't sure which emotion he was projecting.

"Maybe you should think about having a Mia," Needles said. *"No ornery twinsies like Serena has...but a sweet little Mia."*

I laughed. "I'm in my forties, Needles. Plus, Alex already has a grown adult daughter. Between being an aunt to Cayden and Brooke and watching Jayden sometimes, I'm full up on baby mode." I grinned and waggled my eyebrows at him. "Maybe you're the one needing a little Needles, Jr. or Needlesetta around."

Needles snorted. *"Needlesetta. Where do you come up with this stuff, Princess?"*

Stepping inside Eldon's cottage, I used my magic to turn on

the lights. With the absence of sun due to the rainstorm and the heavy foliage of the forest, natural sunlight was lacking.

The cottage was small—the living room and kitchen sharing a cozy, open space. I could make out the remnants of a crackling fire in the fireplace from my vantage point near the door. The walls, plastered and painted a soft, earthen hue, were lined with bookshelves. Walking to one of the shelves, I scanned the books, pictures, and antique toys like the ones in Eldon's shop. But the pièce de résistance was the train track that was suspended with the help of magic and ran the perimeter of the living room. As if sensing someone was inside the house and ready to be amazed, the enchanted train came to life and started to roll down the track, its whistle blowing loudly.

"That's so cool," I whispered.

"He spared no expense," Needles said. *"I can feel the pulse of the magic."*

I nodded. "So can I. It's obvious he loved these vintage toys and took great care with them."

I headed for the kitchen, running my hand along the hand-carved wooden table laden down with more miniature toys, collector magazines, and papers. The glow of an enchanted lantern hanging from one of the wooden beams along the ceiling gave off more than enough light. The kitchen was compact and neatly organized, with copper pots and pans hanging above a stone hearth, and jars of colorful spices and herbs lined the glass-front cabinets.

"I feel like this place really suited the old troll." I gave Needles a small smile, my heart breaking just a little. "Sitting at the table reading his magazines on toys and trains."

"I hate when any supernatural dies," Needles said. *"But this useless killing of an old supernatural just makes me angry."*

"I hear you." I picked up the stack of letters on the kitchen table and started to thumb through them. "Oh, this sounds promising. 'Stop being so selfish. The collection deserves to be on display, not hidden away.' And here's another. 'I know the Supernatural Collectors contacted you. Stop being stubborn, you old fool! It would be a shame if one day they were taken from you and given to others who would appreciate them.' They're all signed from the same person…a Linus Gallion."

"He sounds like a good suspect."

"Parker Stonebridge mentioned overhearing an argument between Eldon and someone named Linus. I bet it's the same guy." I conjured an evidence bag and slipped the papers inside.

"Did this Parker kid give you a description of the guy?"

"Sure did. Let me ward the house, then we can go figure out what to do about Pepper and her kiddos, and then see how Doc and Finn are coming along. Oh, and I want to talk to the woodland animals again real quick."

I stepped outside and warded the house while Needles rounded up Brixlee and Vip.

"Did either of you two see the person walking in the woods looking for the family who was hiding in the log?" I asked. "Could you tell if it was a man or a woman?"

The rabbit and squirrel both shook their heads.

"They were wearing a big coat," Vip said. *"And the hood was big and hid their face. I don't know if it was a man or woman."*

"I'm sorry," Brixlee said. *"It was the same for me. I was so focused on making sure the person didn't find the family, that I didn't think to look at the person's face. I was just running around and stepping over the footprints."*

"You both did great work," I said. "Your actions probably kept the family safe. You two should be proud of what you did here today." I bent down and ran my hands down each of their backs. "I know I'm thankful, and I know my dad, Black Forest King, will be thankful as well when I tell him. You did a great thing volunteering to help out and save another family. Good job, Brixlee. Good job, Vip."

9

Tommy and Pepper were sitting on the hollowed-out log when Needles and I found them a few minutes later. The kids were still playing with some of the woodland animals, running and laughing.

"I appreciate it," Pepper said, "but I still don't think it would look proper."

Tommy threw back his head and laughed. "Honey, I stopped caring what people thought and said about me years ago. You need to feel safe, and Shayla and I want you safe. Besides, technically, I own the cottage now. I don't want anything happening to my property." He winked at her. "Or the people inside the property."

Figuring they were still talking about whether or not Tommy was going to spend the night in her front yard, I decided to put my two cents' worth in. "Do you know how I first met Tommy?"

Pepper shook her head. "No idea."

"My father is a Genus Loci." Her eyes widened, and I smiled. "Yeah, I'm aware how rare that is. Being the daughter of Black

Forest King isn't as great as some people might think. My abilities differ greatly from other magicals. I can communicate with plants and animals. I can even manipulate—well, I'm not sure what you'd call it. Let's just say one time in a fight with the bad guys, I slammed my fists on the ground and the earth shook for miles around. When you're a kid, that kind of oddity can be almost a curse. I was in town one day running from two older werewolf boys who were giving me chase, and Tommy saw. He never said a word, just stepped out from between the buildings where he had been standing, knocked those two boys' heads together, gave them a good shaking, and threw them down the sidewalk." I placed my hand on Tommy's shoulder, something I could do since he was sitting down. "From that day on, we were best friends." I smiled. "Actually, Tommy was pretty much my only friend outside of my cousin Serena. Tommy has a good heart. A big, gentle heart. And he's protective of those who he thinks need protecting. He's like a gargoyle in that sense. I should know, I'm married to a gargoyle."

"You just had to go and ruin a good story by talking about the gargoyle," Needles grumbled.

Pepper stared me in the eyes, her face hard and unyielding. "My children are the most important things to me. I would move heaven and earth to keep them safe. I'm aware some things may come to light because of what has happened to Eldon Stonebridge. While my heart breaks for him, I need to keep my children's safety my number one priority." She stood and faced Tommy. "If you can guarantee me that protection, then I accept your invitation to camp out in my front yard tonight." She stuck out her hand, and still sitting, Tommy shook it. "I appreciate your offer, Mr. Trollman."

Tommy smiled. "Call me Tommy. I'll run into town, grab some things, pick up dinner, and be right back out."

Pepper's eyes went wide, and she shook her head emphatically. "Oh, no. You don't have to get dinner. I can make something from my house."

Tommy slapped his hands on his thighs, his laugh echoing in the forest. "I am a large troll with an even larger appetite. You probably don't have enough food in your cabinets and refrigerator to fill me up, Miss Pepper. Tonight will be my treat. You just let me know what you and the kids like."

Tears sprang in Pepper's eyes, and she blinked them back furiously. "Thank you. That's very generous of you, Tommy."

"Now that that's settled," I said, "I need to get back to the store. I want to see how Doc and Finn are coming along."

Tommy stood and placed a large hand on my shoulder. "I'll check in throughout the night here."

"Appreciate it, Tommy."

Needles and I bid farewell to everyone, including the animals, and hurried back toward Across the Bridge Trinkets. Crossing the moat, I stepped inside the back door and observed Doc and Finn working.

Finn stood when she saw me in the doorway. "There's a lot of broken glass. I'm probably going to have to pull an all-nighter just to get all of these back together again. Even using magic, it will be time-consuming."

"Do you need help?" I asked. "I can come back into town tonight."

Finn waved her hand dismissively in the air. "Oh, no. I've got this. It's just going to be a long night, that's all. I think I may have found the murder weapon, though." She levitated an evidence bag over to me. "Tested positive for blood."

I grabbed the bag and brought it closer to my face. "Definitely heavy enough. A cast iron cauldron? I wonder if the killer brought it with them or if this was in the shop?"

"I think it was in the shop," Finn said. "And I only say that because I found some pennies and other small change on the ground as well. My assumption is Eldon kept loose change in it for customers who needed to either leave a penny or take a penny." She flashed me a grin. "I found that sign as well."

"Makes sense." I handed her back the bag. "So maybe Eldon and the killer got into an altercation. The killer picked up the cauldron in a fit of anger and whacked Eldon upside the head." I looked around the store and spotted the metal fairy Parker had mentioned sitting on the counter. "Where did you find the cauldron? Was it near Eldon's body, or did the killer toss it among all this debris to try to hide it?"

"It was in with all the debris," Finn said. "My guess is the killer was trying to hide it."

"I suppose if he was that methodical, chances are pretty good he may have wiped off the fingerprints as well, but it doesn't hurt to try."

Finn nodded. "Exactly."

I heard a car door slam outside, an engine purr to life, and then the car drive away. "Tommy must be heading back into town. Don't forget to get a mold of the tire tread from outside if you haven't done that already, Finn."

"That's my next stop, Shayla."

I glanced at the ten evidence bags magically suspended above us and shook my head. "Are you sure you can put these pieces back together?"

Finn laughed. "That's the beauty of magic and perseverance."

When she picked up her field kit and walked outside, I turned to Doc, who was standing silently in a corner, arms and legs crossed, watching our exchange. "You okay?"

Doc nodded. "Just keeping out of Finn's way. I've finished examining the body. I'm fairly confident the blow to the temple is what killed him. I'm tentatively placing the time of death between 8:00 and 10:00 this morning. I should be able to get closer when I do the autopsy." He sighed and pushed off the wall. "You'd think I'd be used to this by now. I've been doing this job longer than you've been alive, Shayla. Heck, almost longer than your mother has been alive."

A loud clap of thunder rattled the windows, and I almost jumped. A few seconds later, the sky opened up, and once again, large, heavy raindrops fell at a high rate of speed.

"Finn's cursing the rain and working on the mold, Princess," Needles said as he zipped back inside the store through the open front door. *"It looks like it'll just get worse. The sky is dark as far as I can see."*

"We better start our investigation," I said. "You two got this covered?"

Doc nodded. "We do. Finn can lock up and ward the store."

"Great. We'll talk in the morning."

"I'll be ready to go first thing." He gave me a small smile. "Poor Finn might need more time with the assembling, but we'll have something for you guys."

"Thanks, Doc."

Needles settled on my shoulder, and I walked toward the front door. The temperature had dropped a couple more degrees over the last half hour, making the wind bite and sting even more. I couldn't help but smile as Finn sprinted to the front door, laughing at the rain beating against her body.

"I may need a hot drink and hot shower when I get back to the station," she said as she scooted by me. "You guys stay warm as well."

Needles gave her a snappy salute, then zipped out the front door, wings glowing yellow and pink, straight for the Bronco.

Laughing, I waved my hand in the air and used my magic to

open the passenger-side door for him. Flipping the hood on my slicker over my head, I sprinted to the Bronco as well.

Once inside, I started the engine and pulled out my cell phone. I turned on the heat just enough to take the chill out of the air and called Alex.

"Whaddya know?" Alex asked.

"Got some names for you and Grant to run."

"Got my pen and paper handy."

"Where are you?" I asked.

"Pulled over on the side of the road down by Dolphin Harbour on the south side of the island. I was thinking of running into that little shack by the dock and grabbing some clam chowder."

"Sounds nice and warm. I got six names so far for you to run—Barton Longtree, Gloria and Parker Stonebridge, Dalton Fowler, Linus Gallion, and Pepper Hollis."

Alex chuckled. "You've been busy."

"Listen, I think Pepper Hollis might be like Maggie Castings."

"Maggie?" Alex mused. "The woman who was running from her past and hiding out here on the island?"

Alex and I had met Maggie on a previous case we'd worked.

"Yes. Just a hunch. Don't dig too hard, okay? I don't want to throw up any red flags in case she is running and the person she's running from is still trying to find her. Just whatever PADA has on a Pepper Hollis."

"You don't consider her a suspect?" Alex mused.

"No. But I'd like to know more about her and her situation. I want to know who she's running from."

10

According to the app on my phone, Barton Longtree lived on the south side of town but had his store on the east side over on Stargaze Drive. Since it was just after lunch on a weekday, I figured Barton would be at his store. If he was at his store all morning, depending on what time he opened, I would be hard-pressed to pin the murder on him.

I pulled up to the store and parked along the curb. The rain had let up just a little, but I was still reluctant to get out of the Bronco.

"Looks like there's a note on the door, Princess. I think I'll just stay here where it's nice and warm."

I jogged over to the front door of the store, and sure enough, a note was taped to the glass. Barton had a family emergency and wouldn't be in for the day. Turning around, I dashed back to the Bronco and hopped inside.

"Guess we'll be driving to Barton's house. The shop is closed today due to a family emergency."

"Is killing someone considered a family emergency, Princess?"

Snickering, I dug through my backpack and handed Needles a pretzel rod. "Not the last time I checked."

Pulling up Barton Longtree's home address on my phone app, I pulled onto the street and headed for the south side of town. It took about fifteen minutes longer than usual, thanks to the downed tree branches on Spellbound Street. Luckily, I just used my magic to move them to the side of the road and then left a message with town hall to add it to the long list of debris pick up the island workers were plowing through.

Barton's one-story bungalow was the last house on the right on Mystic Moon Lane. It was in an older section of town, so most of the houses were small and older themselves. The oak tree in the front yard was large enough to give a little shelter as Needles and I dashed up the walkway to the front door.

After my second knock, the door swung open, and a tall, gangly fairy with a long white beard and thinning white hair stared out at me.

"What do you want?" he snapped. "It's nasty out here, and my bones don't like it."

I rubbed my wet hands together, hoping to take away the chill. "Mr. Longtree? My name is Agent Loci-Stone, and this is my partner, Needles. I need to ask you a few questions."

"What kind of questions? And hurry up, it's cold."

"First, I apologize if I have interrupted your family emergency."

He scowled, crossing his arms over his chest. "What are you talking about?"

"Needles and I dropped by Fairy Lights in town and saw your note. It said you had a family emergency?"

"It's raining. I'm an old man. That's emergency enough for me."

I nodded. "I see. Well, do you know an Eldon Stonebridge?"

Barton's nostrils flared, and his eyes narrowed. "I know that weaselly little troll. What about him?"

"He's dead."

Not how I would normally tell someone another person had passed away, but I wanted to gauge Barton's reaction.

Barton's eyebrows rose, and he gave me a half-smile. "You don't say? Well, isn't that a shame?" He shrugged. "Isn't that what you're supposed to say?"

I ignored his question. "Can you tell me the last time you spoke to Mr. Stonebridge?"

"I don't speak to the man unless I have to."

"Okay, when was the last time you were forced to speak to Mr. Stonebridge?"

Barton snorted. "I don't know, maybe a month or so ago. I saw him in a store here in town. We scowled, gave each other the bird, said a few curse words under our breaths, then walked away."

"I see."

"I wish I could've seen it. That had to be hilarious."

"When was the last time you were at his shop?" I asked.

Barton scowled and crossed his arms over his chest. "I ain't never been out to his stupid store. Why would I?"

"Never?" I mused.

"Never!" Barton hissed.

"Can you tell me why you two didn't get along?"

"We were business partners years ago when we were in our twenties." He scowled and looked away. "Anyway, after about five years as partners, we split the business. End of story. Been like over fifty years ago. What's the big deal now?"

Oh, there is no way that was the end of the story. "Why did you guys split?"

Barton shrugged. "I think Eldon called it 'ethical differences' or some crap like that." He put air quotes around ethical differences. "Basically, I wanted to run the business one way, and he wanted to run it another."

"Can you give me an example?"

Barton crossed his arms and scowled. "I thought we should spend the money on more product, but Eldon didn't. So, I took some money and bought more product. He accused me of stealing! Me! It was half my business. I could do what I wanted with some of the money."

"So you guys dissolved your partnership?"

"You're darn right we did! But then that troll went too far!"

"How did he do that?"

"About a year after we split our business, Eldon bought a curse from an old fairy on the east side of the island. That nasty troll, Eldon Stonebridge, cursed me!"

"How do you know he cursed you?"

Barton threw up a hand. "Because bad things started to happen! My wife left me, my new business started losing money, and things started going south, fast." He snickered. "When I asked Eldon about it, he denied it! He said he went to see the fairy for prosperity spells and protection spells for his new business. But I knew he was lying!"

"Who is the fairy, do you know?"

"Doesn't matter now. She's dead. Long dead." A sly grin spread across his face. "Of course, Eldon didn't come away unscathed from that curse. The granddaughter of the old fairy developed a little crush on Eldon. And from what I understand, even after all these years, he still can't shake her."

I blinked in surprise at that. "You're telling me someone had been in love with Eldon for almost fifty or sixty years and neither one ever acted on it?"

"*Talk about unrequited love,*" Needles said, his wings glowing red and blue.

"Oh, she ended up marrying another fairy like ten years later, but he died within the first year of their marriage. But as far as I know, she's been chasing Eldon ever since."

"And what's the fairy's name?" I asked.

"Vera Wingsom."

Wingsom. I knew a few Wingsoms on the island. And Barton was correct, they were powerful fairies.

"Where were you from 8:00 to 10:00 this morning?" I asked.

Barton scowled and crossed his arms over his chest again. "Where do you think I was? Here. It's raining outside, and my bones don't like the rain. Old fairy, remember?"

I took in the man before me. He was older, but I could also see muscles still defined in his upper arms. He actually looked quite strong and healthy to me. "So you were here the entire morning? Never went out?"

"That's right."

"*Oh, you got him now, Princess!*"

"Then when did you put the sign on your door down at the store?"

"*Boom! I believe Zoie would call that a mic drop.*"

I bit back a smile. I was sort of proud of that one myself.

Barton's eyes widened for half a second. "Fine, I went out for a few minutes. Just enough time to drive into town, slap a note on the door before I was supposed to open at 8:00, then came straight home."

"Is there anyone who could vouch for you? Maybe you live with someone? Maybe you spoke with a neighbor?"

"I live with no one, and I definitely don't speak to my neighbors. They'd just want to start yakking every time they saw me, if I did."

"Yes, because he has quite the charming personality."

"What time would you say you left your home this morning?"

"Maybe 7:30, and I returned probably around 8:15 or 8:30."

"But nobody can corroborate that, right?"

Barton narrowed his eyes and frowned. "Are you calling me a liar?"

I could feel Needles vibrating on my shoulder. *"Oh, he's going to want to watch his tone, Princess. I'm itching to carve out someone's tongue today."*

"I'm merely trying to ascertain your alibi," I said calmly.

"Well, I just gave you my alibi." He snapped his fingers. "Wait, I saw my granddaughter and her boyfriend coming out of the Enchanted Island Café around—well, I guess it would have been around 8:15 because I'd already been to my store. They'd just had breakfast. I stopped and talked with them for a few minutes, but then when the rain picked up, we parted ways. I probably got home around 8:30. I made myself some coffee and have been sitting at the table watching the rain ever since. Until you knocked on my door and interrupted me." He snickered. "Not that I'm upset about the reason for the intrusion. In fact, if that's all the questions you've got for me, I think I'm gonna go back inside and raise a toast to the dead Eldon Stonebridge. Worst business partner and friend I ever had. Good riddance."

"What's your granddaughter's name?" I asked.

"Ellie. Ellie Longtree."

That was the second time in a matter of hours I'd heard the name Ellie. No way that could be a coincidence. "Who's her boyfriend?"

Barton shrugged. "I dunno. Some fella by the name of Colton or Walton or something like that."

I was betting money it was Dalton. Dalton Fowler.

"Is the boyfriend an artist?" I asked. "Does he sell items in your store?"

"Yeah. Now that you say that. But not long, he hasn't. Maybe about three or four months. That's why I can't ever remember his name. He ain't been around long, and knowing what a heartbreaker my granddaughter is, I don't figure he'll stay around long, either." He grinned, showing me his crooked teeth. "She takes after her grandpa. Doesn't let anyone get too close."

11

Vera Wingsom lived in a small cul-de-sac subdivision surrounded by a thick forest. There were five other houses on her street, but there was still enough distance and trees to offer a ton of privacy. Her cottage was like many cottages set in the woods—made of stone, rounded windows, and moss growing on the cedar-shake shingles. Her front garden was already sprouting flowers.

As Needles settled on my shoulder, I gave two sharp raps on the wooden door. I heard movement inside, and then a few seconds later the front door was opened by an attractive fairy with silver-blonde hair cut in a chin-length bob, cornflower blue eyes, and a wide smile.

"Hello, dear. How can I—oh, look at you. Aren't you just the most beautiful porcupine?"

"Huh. Whaddya know?"

Exactly what I thought. Everyone always assumed Needles was a hedgehog.

"My name is Agent Loci-Stone. Are you Vera Wingsom?"

The woman's smile reached her eyes, and I almost wanted to kick myself for what I was about to do.

"I am," she said. "Now, I believe from your uniform you are the game warden, but I must admit, I'm a little unsure of why you are here. I don't hunt or do anything that would get me in trouble with the game warden."

I knew it was going to break my heart to have to break hers if what Barton Longtree said was true...that this lovely woman had been in love with Eldon Stonebridge for over fifty years.

"No, ma'am. You are not in trouble. I'm afraid I may have some difficult news for you. Do you—"

The color drained from Vera's face, and she grabbed hold of the doorjamb. "Is it my son? Has something happened to him?"

I shook my head. "No. I am not sure who your son is, but this is not about him. This is about Eldon Stonebridge."

The woman blinked in surprise, then gave a soft laugh. "Oh, Eldon? What about him?"

"You know Eldon Stonebridge?"

A pretty pink blush spread across Vera's cheeks. "Oh, yes. Eldon and I go way back. He's such a dear man."

"As I was saying, I'm afraid I have some difficult news. Eldon Stonebridge's body was discovered at his store earlier this morning."

Vera's eyes went wide, and her chin started to tremble. "What? Eldon? You sure? How? Was he sick?" Tears ran down her cheeks, but she brushed them away and frowned at me. "Wait. How do you know Eldon and I knew each other? What's really going on here?"

I heard the jaunty whistle before I saw the man and woman strolling down the cobblestone path that led from one of the other houses I'd observed on the cul-de-sac. They weren't paying us any attention until they were almost upon us. Cutting off his whistle, the man glanced over to where we stood.

"Vera? What's the matter?" He hurried up the walkway, the woman trailing behind him. "Why are you crying? What's wrong?" He turned to glare at me, but I didn't take offense. "What have you done?"

Before I could say anything, Vera waved her hand in the air. "No, Dalton. Don't be upset with Agent Loci-Stone. It isn't her fault I took the news so hard."

"News? What news?" he demanded. "Vera, tell me what's going on?"

"Yes," the younger woman beside him said. "What's got you so upset?"

"Why don't we start with names," I said. "My name is Agent Loci-Stone, and I'm the game warden for Enchanted Island. This is my partner, Needles. Who are you two?"

"I'm Ellie Longtree, and this is my boyfriend, Dalton Fowler. Dalton is Vera's neighbor. He comes and checks on her at least once a day, right Vera?"

Vera nodded. "Yes. Dalton is such a sweet boy. Why doesn't everyone come in?" Vera stepped back and motioned us inside. "I don't know about you guys, but I could use some hot tea. I just poured a cup before you all arrived."

With one more scathing look, Dalton motioned for me to go ahead of him. I stepped into the living room and looked around. The interior walls were painted a mossy green, with one wall exposing a bit of the stone exterior. A small fireplace crackled and popped, taking off the chill in the room. Petal-shaped wall sconces were the only light in the room outside of the fireplace, and her shelves were packed with plants, trinkets, and books. Woven rugs were thrown across the wooden floors in what seemed like random placements.

"Your home is lovely." I crossed the floor and sat down on a plush green recliner, Needles dropping onto the armrest.

"Can I get you something hot to drink?" Vera asked.

I shook my head. "No, thank you. I'll get something when I get back to town."

Vera and Ellie sat on the flowered sofa while Dalton pulled a chair in from the other room and sat it next to Ellie.

"I'm sorry I reacted like I did," Vera said. "It was just such a surprise." She turned to Dalton and Ellie. "I'm afraid I have some upsetting news."

The man frowned. "What?"

"Eldon Stonebridge is dead," Vera whispered.

The man reared back, his eyes wide. "Seriously? Dead? You're sure?"

Vera nodded and rested a hand on her chest. "That's why I'm so upset."

"Whoa," Ellie murmured. "My grandpa is going to freak out."

"Well, damn." Dalton ran his hands through his hair and sighed. "I'm sorry, Vera. I know you seemed to like the guy a lot. How did he die?"

"We haven't gotten the autopsy back yet," I said, "but we suspect foul play."

Vera and Ellie both gasped, and Dalton's eyes went wide.

"You mean like he was murdered?" Dalton asked.

I nodded. "Perhaps. Did you know Eldon Stonebridge too?"

Dalton nodded. "Yeah. I sell some of my creations in his shop."

"You're an artist?" I mused. "What do you sell?"

"Wind chimes, lawn ornaments, that kind of stuff. I make it all in my shed behind my house."

"He's very talented," Ellie said. "He sells his creations in a couple different stores on the island."

I studied the three supernaturals carefully before asking my next question. "Dalton, we've had a witness state they heard you arguing with Eldon Stonebridge awhile back. They thought it was about a price increase or percentage increase? Does that ring a bell?"

Dalton nodded. "Yes. One of the times I went in last month to drop off more wind chimes and lawn decorations, Eldon told me he'd be taking more from my split."

"So unfair," Ellie said.

"What was your split at the time?" I asked.

"He got thirty, and I got seventy. He said he'd be taking forty now." He lifted one hand and shrugged. "I'm not going to deny I was angry. It just came out of the blue. No warning at all. And that's a pretty substantial cut into my profits."

"So you two argued?" I pushed.

"I guess you could say that. In the end, he told me if I wasn't happy, I could take my things and walk. I chose to stay."

"And this was a little over a month ago?"

Dalton nodded, then glanced at Ellie. "I think he somehow found out I was selling my stuff at Fairy Lights, and I know there's bad blood there between Eldon and Ellie's granddad."

Ellie nodded. "It's true there's bad blood, but it's also true he shouldn't have taken a higher percentage from you."

Dalton shrugged. "I'm still selling at three other shops on the island as well, so hopefully it won't be too noticeable over time."

"And one of those shops is Fairy Lights, correct?" I asked. "The shop Barton Longtree owns?"

Dalton nodded. "Yes. But that's a recent development." He glanced at Ellie. "Just a couple months, right?"

She nodded. "That sounds right."

"It's still such a small world," Vera murmured.

I leaned forward in my seat and caught Vera's eyes. "How did you first meet Eldon?"

Vera gave me a soft smile. "He used to come by my grandmother's house for potions, charms, and elixirs when he needed them. I was seventeen the first time I met him." She looked at Ellie and smiled wistfully. "I've never really talked about this before, especially since I know who Ellie is. But when Eldon first opened his business with Barton Longtree some fifty-something years ago, he had my grandmother make him prosperity charms and good-luck charms for their business. He did this for a few years. Then, when I was probably twenty-one, he came by and asked my grandmother for a separation charm and a truth charm." She lowered her head. "I'm a little ashamed to say I eavesdropped on their conversation when he came to her that day." Her cheeks went pink. "But I really liked Eldon, and I wanted to know why he was so upset. He told my grandmother he and Barton were separating their business because of unethical practices, and he needed some charms to keep him safe and free from retaliation."

Ellie scoffed. "My grandpa said Eldon bought a curse from your grandmother."

Vera shook her head, her hair falling softly around her face. "That's not true, Ellie. My grandmother was *not* that kind of fairy." She sighed. "This is why I never talk about Eldon or your grandpa when you come to visit with Dalton. I don't want to bring up hard feelings."

I cleared my throat. "So you've known Eldon Stonebridge for a good many years, Vera?"

"Oh, yes." She blinked back tears. "I knew Eldon for a very long time."

"And she obviously cared about the man," Needles said, his wings glowing pink and purple. *"You can see it still today."*

"Were you in love with him?" I asked gently.

Vera laughed softly and covered her face with one hand. "Oh, my no."

But something in her tone had Dalton leaning over to stare at her. "Is that why you'd sometimes ask to tag along with me to his shop, Vera?" He snorted. "I just thought you wanted to get out of the house. I didn't realize it was because you wanted to see Eldon."

"Of course not." Vera gave a small laugh. "Don't be silly." She bit her lip and blinked back the tears that suddenly sprang in her pretty blue eyes. "Well, maybe. I'd always hoped he might see me as someone other than the young girl he first met all those years ago."

"Vera," I mused, "when was the last time you saw Eldon?"

"Oh, it's been at least three months. I used to go in with Dalton quite a bit to help him restock some of his items. But once Dalton started dating Ellie, I stopped accompanying him. Ellie does that now with Dalton."

"You should have said something, Vera," Ellie said. "I may not have liked the guy, but I didn't mean to keep you two apart."

Vera waved her hand in the air. "Oh, it's no big deal, Ellie."

But I wasn't so certain.

"She's totally lying, Princess."

"You've been married before, Vera?" I asked.

Vera nodded. "Yes. It was the right thing to do. And I cared for him, honest. We were married a little over a year, and I was about four months pregnant, when he was diagnosed with Eclipse Heart—a rare disease that causes a vampire's heart to slowly crystalize. He died before our son was born. I decided to go back to my maiden name. I didn't want the constant reminder that I was a young widow. Plus, my family was well-known on the island, and I love the Wingsom name."

I nodded. "Understandable. And I'm sorry for your loss."

"Thank you."

"And you, Dalton?" I asked. "When was the last time you saw or spoke to Eldon?"

"I saw him last week at his shop. Nothing out of the ordinary. We just talked about what was new on the island. I replenished my stock, he gave me a check, and then I left."

I nodded. "Okay. Dalton, where were you this morning from 8:00 to 10:00?"

Dalton's eyes went wide before he schooled his features. "Ellie spent the night, so we decided to go out for breakfast. We ate at Enchanted Island Café, and then we came back here. Ellie works from home, so it doesn't matter where she's at physically. She decided to stay here and work. So when she shut the door at 9:00, I went out to my shed to work on my own things. We didn't see each other again until I went inside to grab a late lunch. Ellie gets an hour. So after a quick bite, we decided to walk down here to check on Vera. With all this rain, I wanted to make sure her house was still leak free."

Vera smiled. "I don't know how I got so lucky, Dalton, when you moved in down the lane all those years ago."

I turned to Ellie. "Does that account sound right to you?"

Ellie nodded. "Yeah. We had breakfast in town, and then we came home. I hate to hurry this along, but I really do have to get back on my computer within the next twenty minutes, or I'll be docked pay."

"Understood," I said. "When you were in town this morning, did you see anyone or talk to anyone?"

Ellie nodded. "Yeah. We saw my granddad. He was coming

from his store. He said it was too nasty outside to stay open. He was going home to stay dry."

"What time was that?" I asked.

Ellie shrugged and looked at Dalton. "I don't know. It was after we ate. So maybe 8:15 or 8:30? I don't start work until 9:00, so I know it was before that. We drove home from town, and I still had plenty of time to start up my laptop and get to work."

"Who do you work for?" I asked.

"Supernatural Insurance Underwriters," Ellie said. "They're based outside of Boston in a supernatural town."

"I don't understand," Vera said. "Are you saying Dalton and Ellie are suspects? Why?"

I sighed. "I'm going to need your alibi as well, Ms. Wingsom."

Vera's mouth dropped. "Mine? You think *I* might have killed Eldon?" She held up both hands. "I had feelings for him. Why would I hurt him?" Her chin trembled, and a tear slipped down her cheek. "Why would anyone hurt him for that matter?"

"I'm just doing my job and covering all the bases," I said softly. "Plus, it also helps me eliminate people. Can you please tell me where you were this morning, Vera?"

For a second, Vera sat quietly and gathered herself. Finally, she cleared her throat. "I had a coffee and croissant with two other women this morning at Enchanted Bakery and Brew. I'm sure the women who own the bakery will vouch for us. We were there for close to an hour. Maybe 8:00 to 9:00?"

"That'll be easy to verify, Princess."

"And then afterward?" I asked.

"I came home. It was maybe 9:15? But I don't have anyone who can verify that. I didn't know I'd need to have an alibi handy. Otherwise, I'd have checked in with friends or something."

Ellie reached over and patted Vera's hand. "Don't worry, Vera. You did nothing wrong, so you don't have anything to worry about."

Vera smiled half-heartedly at Ellie. "Thank you, dear."

"Ellie is right," I said. "I just need to establish a timeline for everyone involved."

Vera forced a smile and nodded. "Okay. Is there anything else we can help you with?"

I turned to Dalton. "Just one more thing. I assume you weren't the only vendor Eldon was taking a bigger percentage from. Anyone else come to mind who might have a beef with Eldon?"

"I only know of three or four other vendors who sell in the shop," Dalton said, "but I honestly don't know who they are. I've never met any of them. I think one of them is a woman, though. The back door was open one day when I came by, and I could hear Eldon outside laughing. I heard a woman's voice, but couldn't make out their words. I finished restocking, and by the time I was done, he came back in carrying a basket of jams. I asked him who he was talking to, and he said it was just another vendor." A muscle jumped in his jaw. "Between us, I doubt her percentage was cut like mine."

"What makes you say that?" I asked.

Dalton winced, then smiled apologetically at Vera. "The way Eldon was smiling when he came back in. That's not the smile of a guy who is chatting with an old friend, if you know what I mean?"

"She lives in his extra cottage," Ellie said.

"Excuse me?" I asked.

"The woman Dalton is talking about," Ellie said, "my grandfather told me he heard it was some young woman with kids. Eldon set her up in the extra cottage he had."

Vera's eyes filled with sorrow...and jealousy. "She has to be young enough to be his granddaughter. Why? All he ever had to do was look my way, but he never did."

"I don't like the fact they all know about Pepper and the kids," Needles said, his wings glowing gray and blue.

I nodded, agreeing with him.

Dalton snapped his fingers, bringing me out of my thoughts. "I do know Eldon had some collectibles that might be worth something. He kept them behind a magically locked glass cabinet. Maybe someone saw them and tried to rob him and that's how he was killed? Eldon loved those collectibles. I remember asking about one of them, and he went into this hour-long monologue about it." He chuckled. "I never asked again."

"Dalton," Vera scolded gently. "I'm sure he was just excited to talk about them."

"It was an hour, Vera. On one action figure." He looked at me and shrugged. "I'm sorry I can't help you out more. I just didn't know the other vendors."

"He had a niece and great-nephew," Vera said. "He'd talk about them sometimes when I would go with Dalton to restock his products. I don't think they've been on Enchanted Island long."

Dalton waggled a finger. "That's right. The boy has a weird name. Zipper or something like that."

Ellie giggled. "Stone. He makes zipper pulls with stones in them." She looked at me and rolled her eyes. "He corned me outside of Across the Bridge Trinkets to tell me all about his zipper pulls. I suggested he visit my grandpa's store to see if maybe it would be something my grandpa would want to sell." She flashed me a grin. "I knew my grandpa would say no, but I also knew my grandpa would get a kick out of *telling* Eldon Stonebridge's relative no. He still has a grudge, even after all these years." The smile fell from her face. "Or had a grudge, I guess. Seems silly now."

"I got one of those zipper pulls too," Vera said. "Most ridiculous thing ever." She glanced down at her dress clothes. "I wouldn't even know where to put it."

Ellie grinned. "Yeah, you don't exactly wear a lot of clothes with zippers on them, Vera."

I stood, and Needles flew to my shoulder. "Thank you for your time." I handed them each a business card. "If you think of anything that might help me in the investigation, please call."

Vera nodded and sniffed. "I'm very sorry about Eldon. He was always such a nice man."

12

"The bakery's gonna close in about half an hour," I said when we got back in the Bronco. "Let's stop by and talk with Serena, grab something warm to eat and drink, and then go interview Linus Gallion."

"*Sounds good to me, Princess. I think I'll close my eyes and practice my interview technique.*"

I snorted. "Good one."

I sent a quick text to Alex to add Vera Wingsom to the suspect list.

It took a little longer than normal to reach town thanks to a mudslide blocking half the road. Traffic wasn't something to worry about most days on Enchanted Island, but when you only have one lane to drive down, it can be a hassle. And knowing how backed up island workers were, I took matters into my own hands. It took me, two other witches, and a fairy to move all the debris—tree limbs, muddy soil, tree roots, and rocks—off the road. By the time I got back in the Bronco, I was soaked to my bones and miserable.

Enchanted Bakery and Brew was just about empty when Needles and I finally entered. Gertrude Anise and Beverly Sage were the only customers, and they were so engrossed in their conversation, I was almost past them before they waved hello.

"We were just talking about poor Eldon," Gertrude said. "Such a shame. He was one of the nice ones."

"And his store had just the right eclectic merchandise," Beverly added. "It was just too bad it was so far out of the way."

"Did either of you know him well?" I asked.

Both ladies shook their heads.

"The troll kept to himself," Gertrude said. "Sorry we can't be of more help."

I waved goodbye to the two witches and headed for the display case where Serena and Tamara stood. In the far corner, Jayden Sparks sat coloring and chatting with Cayden and Brooke —both of whom were in car seats and looked to be sleeping.

"You have Jayden today?" I asked Tamara.

She smiled and glanced over at the little girl who would be officially hers next week. The adoption would go through well before the wedding ceremony, which is what everyone had hoped for. "Yeah, I knew the twins would be here, and I thought maybe Zac's aunt and uncle could use a break."

"She's great with the twins," Serena said. "She's very patient. She'll make a fantastic big sister one day."

Tamara's face flushed, and she waved a hand at Serena. "Oh, hush. There's plenty of time for that."

"We heard about Eldon Stonebridge," Serena said. "Are you investigating?"

"You bet we are. He died surrounded by a body of water. Therefore, he's our jurisdiction."

"We argued and won our case," I said.

Serena grinned. "Oh, I bet that went over well." She leaned in close, her eyes twinkling. "Tell me, how mad was Alex?"

I laughed. "He wasn't mad at all. In fact, he made it sound like we would be helping him out. All this rain is causing tons of downed trees, mudslides, roof leaks, and lots of other problems for citizens. I think he, Grant, and Deputy Sparks have their hands full as it is." I clapped my hands together. "Anyway, Needles and I are heading to the northwest side of town to interview a person of interest." I glanced down at the display case. "Looks like I'll be taking that cranberry oatmeal cookie and that chocolate croissant."

"Sorry about that, Shayla," Tamara said. "The townspeople swarmed us this morning, and we were almost completely sold out by lunchtime."

I waved her apology away with my hand. "Don't apologize. It's great you guys almost sold out. Although, you're going to have to work twice as hard tomorrow to replenish everything."

The two women exchanged looks.

"We were just talking about that," Serena said. "Weather forecast just moved the tropical storm up to a Category One hurricane. Seems the winds are picking up out in the ocean."

"But that won't happen until tomorrow around 4:00," Tamara said. "So we should be tucked in safe at our homes by then if we decide to open."

Serena nodded. "I say we pare down in the morning to the basics of breads, cookies, and muffins. We'll worry about tarts and cupcakes and those kinds of things after the storm clears."

I moaned. "Homemade bread and stew sounds fabulous."

"And caramel-dipped pretzel rods," Needles said, his wings glowing purple and green. *"Don't forget about those."*

Serena laughed. "As if we could. And before you ask, don't

worry, we saved you one for today just in case you guys stopped by."

Tamara turned, and using her magic, levitated a hidden pretzel rod from under the counter. "We didn't want some kid coming in and buying it."

"You ladies are the best. My favorite witches today." He grabbed the rod and zipped over to where the kids were gathered at the table by the window.

"I don't know what you have planned for dinner," Serena said, heading toward the back kitchen. "But we do have one more item back here."

I wrung my hands together in anticipation. Whatever it was, I would be more than happy to take it off their hands. I didn't have long to wait before Serena returned.

"Here you go," Serena said. "Tamara and I have been trying our hands at painted sourdough bread."

Serena turned the top of the round sourdough ball toward me, and I gasped. "That's absolutely beautiful. We're supposed to eat that?"

Serena and Tamara laughed so hard, Gertrude and Beverly stopped talking to look over at us.

"Yes," Tamara said. "You're supposed to eat that."

It looked like an artistic masterpiece with daisies and other colorful wildflowers across the top, complete with green leaves. "These are going to be huge sellers."

"That's what we're hoping for," Serena said.

Tamara slid a large coffee across the countertop. "Figured you could use this as well."

"Before I leave," I said. "I have a quick question. I spoke to Vera Wingsom earlier. She's a fairy. She said she was in here this morning around eight with two other fairies. I don't suppose you'd remember three older ladies in here this morning, would you? Vera has silver-blonde hair cut to her chin. Beautiful blue eyes."

"Vera and her lady friends come in once a month," Serena said. "I remember them coming in. They usually stay about forty minutes. Sometimes they—oh, wait. I might have a copy of their receipt. Hold on."

"I'll go get it," Tamara said.

I made small talk with Serena until Tamara came back, holding a receipt. "Looks like we rang her out around 8:52. Does that help?"

I nodded and gathered my goodies off the counter. "Sure does. Thanks."

I called to Needles, and we said goodbye to everyone in the bakery. Placing my fancy sourdough bread on the passenger-side seat, I barely refrained from buckling it in with my seatbelt. I thought that might be taking it a little too far.

But just barely.

13

Linus Gallion lived in a two-story older apartment complex on the northwest side of town. It was small, with only eight apartments in the entire building. The exterior stucco had seen better days, but the walkways and bushes were upkept and taken care of.

Linus' apartment was on the second floor, according to the information on my phone app. Snickering just a little at the whimsy, I used the Yoda doorknocker attached to Linus' front door. I couldn't help myself. It was just too cool to pass up.

A large brown eye behind glasses peeked out at me from the slit in the door. "What's the password?"

"I like to carve out tongues," Needles deadpanned. *"That would be my password."*

I bit my lips to keep from laughing out loud. "My name is Agent Loci-Stone. I need to speak to Linus Gallion."

"That's me."

The door was still just cracked, and I could only make out his eyeball. "Mr. Gallion, may I come in, please?" When he made no move to open the door, I dropped the other shoe. "Or we can take this downtown and do a formal interview, if you'd like?"

Another pause...then the door shut, and I heard the sound of multiple locks and chains fall away. How many locks did he have on the door? Five or six? What was he hiding in there? Parker had said he was a witch, so unless he was a normal, he'd be able to ward his place as well. Why all the added security?

He stepped back and motioned us inside. "Please don't touch anything. I don't like people touching my collection."

Linus Gallion was just over six feet tall, stringy dark hair that fell to his round shoulders, and skin so pale I thought he might burst into flames if he went outside. When he pushed his round black glasses up his nose, I was pretty sure this was the witch Parker Stonebridge had seen arguing with Eldon.

Linus eyed Needles and frowned. "He's housetrained, right?"

"Why you little..." Needles leaped from my shoulder, his wings glowing red and orange as he whipped out two quills from his back. *"I'll show you housetrained!"*

"Simmer down, Needles," I said, before he could inflict some damage. "I'm sure he didn't mean to be insulting."

"I was merely asking a pertinent question," Linus said. "My Ms. P is housetrained." He pointed to a massive Pac-Man cathouse across the room. "Aren't you, Ms. P?"

All the drapes were drawn, making the room dark...but not dark enough I couldn't see a yellow cat with a red bow on her head inside the Pac-Man cathouse. Ms. P didn't even glance up at her name. I couldn't blame her, though. I'd freeze out the person who put a bedazzled bow on my tiny head too.

"Please let me run him through with my quills, Princess?"

I glanced around the living room, taking it all in. There was a half-naked Princess Leia cutout in the corner, which was a little off putting. But overall, the living room could double as a gaming sanctuary. I counted five different gaming consoles, a high-end computer complete with three flat-screen monitors, an ergonomic gaming chair, and what I assumed were quality surround sound speakers. Posters of iconic video games and movie characters adorned the walls. The only light—outside of that coming from the flat-screens—was from a hanging Pac-Man light.

Since there was only one chair in the living room, I didn't bother trying to make him comfortable by sitting and chatting. He didn't seem the type, anyway. "Linus, do you know Eldon Stonebridge?"

A muscle twitched in Linus' jaw as he crossed his arms over his chest. "Insufferable, selfish man."

"How do you know him?" I asked.

"He has one of the most extensive collections of both movie and video game action figures I've ever seen. And action figures aren't the only rare memorabilia he has, either."

Putting my hands behind my back, I strolled over to a crammed bookshelf. It was an impressive array of action figures and limited edition collectibles from video games, movies, and comics. Some I recognized…some I didn't.

"Even more impressive than your collection?" I asked.

Linus nodded, his hair moving with him. "Much more impressive."

"His collection is worth a lot of money, then?"

Linus snorted and shoved his glasses up his nose. "I'll say. And he just has them sitting out in his store. It's an expensive, extravagant collection that deserves to be showcased. I just wish he'd listen to me and do something more than just keep them hidden. There are a lot of supernaturals who would love to see those rare items."

"When was the last time you spoke to Eldon Stonebridge?"

"Why?" he demanded. "What's going on?"

"Eldon's body was found earlier this morning. He'd been killed."

Linus took a step back, his already pale skin losing what little color it had. "What about his collection? Is it safe? Did somebody get it?" He fisted his hands in his hair and pulled. "Did somebody get their hands on the collection?"

I shake my head. "No. The collection is still safe."

Linus staggered over and sat down in his ergonomic chair. "Oh, thank goodness. I almost blacked out at the thought of all those beautiful action figures missing."

"Never mind the dead troll. I don't like him, Princess. Let's arrest him and throw away the key."

"You weren't happy with Eldon hiding away his treasures, were you?"

Linus jumped up from the chair. "Would you be? If someone you knew had rare, valuable, one-of-a-kind items, would you be happy if they just hid them away? Not letting anyone else bask in their glory?"

"It's theirs to do with whatever they want," I said. "Eldon had every right to keep his collectables locked away."

"It's not fair!"

"This witch is seriously off his rocker."

"Where were you this morning between 8:00 and 10:00?"

"I was at the post office at 8:00. I sold off a Star Trek action figure on sBay to Ilovest58."

"What?" I had no idea what this guy was saying.

"sBay. You know, the equivalent to what humans call eBay? Anyway, Ilovest58 bought it, and I had to ship it out immediately."

"Okay. So you were at the post office around 8:00? Then where did you go?"

"Ran to the grocery store and picked up a couple snacks. This rain is out of control. It's a good day to stay in and have a Lord of the Rings marathon and play some RPG."

"Some what?" I asked.

He rolled his eyes. "Role-playing games."

"Do you still have your receipt from the grocery store?"

Snatching his wallet off the counter, he opened the middle, yanked out a white receipt, and handed it to me. Check out time at the grocery store was 8:57...which would still give him plenty of time to drive out to Eldon's store and kill him.

Handing him back the receipt, I strolled over to where Ms. P was lounging. I was about to see what Ms. P could tell me. *"Hello, Ms. P. Can you hear me?"*

Ms. P opened one eye and looked up at me. *"Well, isn't that something?"*

"Linus says he went out this morning," I said. *"Is that true?"*

"I suppose it is." She yawned hugely, giving me a glimpse of her sharp teeth.

"Do you know what time he came back home?"

Ms. P glared at me...like only a cat could do. *"Do I look like I know how to tell time?"*

"A simple yes or no will do, Cat!" Needles growled as he zipped over to us, his wings glowing red and purple.

"Then, no. I have no idea." Extending her claws, she reached out and grabbed a power-up mushroom cat toy. *"Now, if you'll excuse me, I have a cat toy to destroy."*

"Well, that was productive," I grumbled as I strolled back over to Linus...who was now busy making sure his action figures were lined up just right on the bookshelf. Reaching into my pocket, I dug out my phone. "Do these letters look familiar?"

Linus glanced down at my phone. "Yes. I sent them to Eldon."

"They sound threatening."

Linus shrugged. "Maybe. I just wanted him to understand how valuable his collection was and how he shouldn't just hide it away."

"Is that really any of your business?" I mused. "I mean, it's his collection."

Linus' face turned red and his nostrils flared. "A collection he didn't deserve! He bought them just to hide them away from the world. A collection like that should be admired."

"By you?" I asked.

"Yes! I'd have loved to talk about them with him. But every time I stopped by the store, he cloaked the glass somehow. I don't know how he did it. He wasn't a magical. He must have paid a witch or fairy a pretty penny to enact a continual magic like that." He frowned. "What will happen to his collection? Do you know?"

"I have no idea. So you knew he kept the valuables behind the glass cabinet in his store?"

"Of course. Why?"

"It looked like someone tried to pry open the cabinet."

Linus scowled and pushed his glasses up his nose. "Well, it wasn't me."

Nodding, I handed him my business card. "Just in case you remember something I need to know."

The minute Linus' front door closed at my back, I strode down the dimly lit hallway of his apartment complex. When I reached the main lobby doors, I made sure Needles was safely tucked next to my neck and threw the hood of my rain slicker over the two of us.

"Let's go see what Pepper and Tommy are up to." I pushed the lobby doors open and hurried outside.

14

"How's everything going?" I asked Pepper Hollis. "You holding up okay?"

We were both standing at the window, watching Tommy, Needles, Jacob, and Mia put up a tent outside in the front yard. Tommy looked to be in his element, laughing and showing Jacob where to strike the hammer. He was a lot more trusting than I, letting a kid near his hand with a hammer.

"I told him again he didn't have to stay," Pepper whispered. "But he insisted. He laughed and said no one would miss him for one night."

"I would say he's correct."

Pepper turned and gave me a small smile. "I don't know how to say this to you. Just know, I'm not running from the law, but I am running."

I nodded. "I figured. You're not the only woman on Enchanted Island who has come here for safety."

Pepper's eyes widened. "Really?"

"Really."

Pepper crossed her arms over her chest, still facing me. "I was married." She gave a harsh laugh. "Heck, maybe I still am? I don't know. I let the ladies helping me escape take care of that. Truth is, I have no plans to ever marry again, so as long as he can't find me, I don't want to make any waves about my marital status."

I nodded. "Okay."

"As far as my husband goes…well, let's just say it was tough in the house when it became apparent Jacob was a normal." She closed her eyes, and a tear ran down her cheek. "But when Mia came along, and she showed tremendous magical abilities, it got even worse. At first, it was just the freezing out. He wanted nothing to do with Jacob. He had no time for him. But when the anger and violence started, that's when I knew I had to take my children and run." She cleared her throat. "My ex-husband was not only wealthy, but he was a prominent member of the town I lived in. He held a high-ranking position. It took a lot to secure what I needed to run. The fairies who helped me knew they would probably be targeted and incur his wrath, but they were willing to go that extra mile because they saw what he was doing."

I placed my hand on her arm. "I got the impression Jacob was a normal, but I wasn't sure. And being a normal is nothing to be ashamed of. In fact, I have a friend you might want to talk to. Until a week or two ago, she was a normal. She lived thirty-something years with no magical abilities. She's getting married in a couple of weeks, but I'm sure if I give her your name and number, she'd love to talk with you."

"So many questions running through my head."

I laughed. "Yes, Devona has quite the story to tell. But it's her story to tell."

Pepper nodded. "Okay"

I caught sight of Jacob and Mia sprinting for the front door, Tommy and Needles trailing behind.

"Mom!" Jacob yelled as he pushed open the front door. "We're done putting up the tent, and now we're thirsty."

"Thirsty!" Mia echoed. "Mommy, thirsty!"

Pepper chuckled. "Well, then I guess I better get everyone something to drink." She glanced up at Tommy as he closed the front door. "Would you like something?"

"Whatever you're giving them is fine," he said.

Pepper grinned. "They're getting elderberry juice."

Tommy grinned back at her. "Elderberry juice sounds delicious."

I turned away and dialed Devona's number while Pepper and the others headed for the kitchen. I quickly filled Devona in on what was going on, and she assured me she would be more than happy to come out tomorrow and talk with Pepper.

I disconnected and hurried into the kitchen. Pepper, Tommy, Jacob, and Mia were all at the table drinking their juice and munching on apple slices, while Needles chewed on a pretzel stick. He looked up guiltily at me when I strode into the room.

"Tommy saw them in the cabinet and told her it was my favorite. It's too bad you didn't marry him instead of the gargoyle."

I narrowed my eyes at Needles before striding to the table and leaning against the counter. "I just spoke to Devona. If it's okay with you, she'd like to come out here tomorrow and just talk. She's like Tommy. Another good one. You can trust her."

"I'd like that," Pepper whispered. "I haven't had another female to talk to since I moved to the island a year ago."

"Devona is a kind soul," Tommy said. "I'm sure you will like her. If she's coming out tomorrow, maybe I'll run into town midmorning and check on things, and then I can be back out later that evening. Maybe come in around four? I can sleep outside again and bring dinner so you don't have to cook."

Pepper's cheeks turned pink, and she glanced down at the table. "Oh, that isn't necessary, Tommy. I'm sure I can find something here that we can all eat. The kids really enjoy chicken strips, so we usually have those and either a vegetable or fruit for our nightly meal."

Jacob nodded glumly. "Every meal."

"Sorry to say it's what I brought out for tonight's meal as well." Tommy winked at Jacob. "But if you could have something else, what would you like?"

"Noodles!" Jacob shouted. "And mac & cheese."

"Oodles!" Mia echoed. "And cheese!"

Tommy laughed. "Then it's settled. If it's okay with your mom, I'll just bring a hodgepodge of stuff tomorrow night, and we can snack on whatever?"

Cheeks still pink, Pepper gave Tommy a small smile. "If you're sure? That'll be two nights in a row you brought out dinner."

"I'm sure," Tommy insisted.

Pepper glanced at her excited children before responding. "Okay, then. That would be lovely."

Tommy nodded once. "It's settled then. Noodles, and mac n' cheese, and whatever else I decide to buy."

"Yay!" Jacob cried, jumping up and down on his butt.

"Yay!" Mia echoed.

But I could tell she wasn't sure what she was cheering for. It was absolutely adorable. I pushed off the counter. "Pepper, you have my phone number if you need anything. Of course, with Tommy sleeping in the front yard, I don't think you're going to have anything to worry about. I'll keep you guys updated throughout the day tomorrow." I glanced at Needles, who was still stuffing his face with pretzels. "You ready to go?"

Needles's wings glowed green and purple as he shot off the counter and landed on my shoulder. *"I hope the gargoyle is making something good for dinner. I'm starving."*

15

"I've got homemade bread!" I shouted as I bolted through the front door of my castle, shaking the rain off my slicker. Seeing the towel on the tile floor in the foyer, I slipped out of my jacket and used my magic to hang it suspended in the air, over the towel. Hurrying into the kitchen, I took a moment to appreciate the wonderful smell coming from within. "And just my luck, something smells delicious."

Alex turned from the stove and grinned. "I grabbed some extra soup from the chowder stand on the south side of the island. I thought it would be the perfect meal for tonight. But if you have homemade bread, that will definitely top it off." He pointed to a glass of white wine on the counter. "I thought we'd do some Riesling tonight."

"Bless you. It's still coming down pretty good out there. I'd like to get nice and warm before going out to see Dad."

"I wondered if we would go tonight, Princess," Needles said as he dropped down onto the counter.

"Might as well," I said, picking up the glass of wine. "He

needs to know what's going on, and then we can do some stakeouts afterward."

Alex arched an eyebrow. "Stakeouts? As in more than one?"

I took a drink of the Riesling and took a moment to appreciate its goodness. "Yes. We will need to do at least one stakeout, maybe two. And then I'd like to check in on Tommy."

"Tommy? What's going on there?" Alex turned on the oven. "In case we want the bread warmed."

Taking the homemade bread out of the bag, I set it on the counter for Alex to see. "Isn't it gorgeous? I almost hate to eat it."

"That *is* spectacular. And you can eat it even though it's painted?"

I laughed. "It's food coloring gel. Perfectly safe to eat."

"I'll stick with my pretzels."

Alex tossed the bread into the oven to warm for a few minutes, and I told Alex about Tommy sleeping overnight in the front yard.

"It's supposed to rain all night," Alex said. "That man is either gonna catch his death of cold, or he's gonna wake up soaking wet."

I smiled. "Pepper's got some magic in her. I'm sure she'll make sure he stays nice and warm. And if she's too shy to offer, then that's one of the reasons why I want to stop by later tonight. Just to check on him."

As Alex dished up the soup, I took the sourdough bread out of the oven and cut it into big chunks. Carrying our meal to the table, I topped off our glasses of wine, and we ate in silence. It wasn't until we pushed our empty bowls away that we finally spoke again.

"That's some of the best chowder I've ever had," I said. "And this bread is just as amazing. I wonder if Zoie is getting in on the sourdough bread kick?"

Alex smiled. "I'm due to talk with her in about ten minutes. I'll ask her." With Zoie still at PADA headquarters and going through the detectives' training program, we hadn't seen her in almost four months. Although, Alex did get to video chat with her quite often.

A loud clap of thunder outside made me groan. "We better head out now, Needles."

"Are you sure you don't want me to fly you out there?" Alex asked.

"Nope. You stay here and talk with Zoie. Come get us in an hour." My cell rang. Digging it out of my pocket, I put it on speakerphone. "Hey, Finn. What's up?"

"I found something in the debris and broken glass that doesn't seem to fit. Could be it just fell off someone's clothing, and it means nothing. But I thought I'd let you know."

"I'll take anything you can give me," I said.

"I found a zipper pull. Looks like there's an onyx stone in the tab. Like I said, could be it fell off a piece of clothing from some customer, or it might be a clue. Dusted for fingerprints and found a partial. Not sure if I'll get a hit, but I'm running it through the database right now. Since it's a partial, it might take longer than normal."

"This is great, Finn. The zipper pull is a clue, and I know what it means. Thanks."

"My pleasure. I've been at this for a while now. I plan on having a late dinner with Jordan, and then coming back tonight to work on putting the pieces together as best I can."

"Are you sure you don't need help?" I asked.

"Nope. I got this. Just be here in the morning, and hopefully I'll have something more for you."

"Thanks, Finn."

I disconnected and smiled at Alex. "That zipper pull could only belong to Parker Stonebridge. He told us he hadn't seen Eldon is a month. I can't believe that zipper pull was never swept up or discovered in that time." I shook my head and stood from the table. "Nope. I think maybe Parker left behind a clue."

Alex grinned. "I take it we're watching him tonight?"

"Yep." I leaned down and kissed him. "See you in an hour."

Ten minutes later, with Needles tucked warmly inside my pocket, I found myself jogging past Mom's cottage. Through a window, I could see her silhouette in the kitchen making her nightly cup of hot tea. She must have been out to see Dad earlier.

Just when I was beginning to think the rainstorm would keep the fireflies away, a familiar ball of light came barreling toward me. Smiling, I waited patiently for it to break apart and the chaos to ensue from the dozen or so lightning bugs.

"Oh, Princess. Can you believe this rain?"

"Black Forest King says a bigger storm is coming."

"Some woodland creatures are coming to Black Forest for shelter."

"Your mom was here, but we walked her home."

"I bet cotton candy would melt in this rain."

On and on they went as I quickly took out a piece of cotton candy from my pocket and watched as they squealed and tore into it. The sugary goodness didn't even have a chance to melt in the rain.

"Follow us, Princess!"

"That was delicious!"

"Where's Needles?"

I answered their questions as we jogged toward the entrance to Black Forest. My favorite pine tree was standing guard like he had since my birth.

"Princess. Black Forest King is waiting for you. It's always a pleasure when you are here." He lifted one of his heavy branches near the ground, and as I ducked down underneath, Needles popped out of my pocket.

"Stop your yammering," he said to the fireflies. *"You're giving me a headache."*

The fireflies squealed with excitement at the sight of Needles, and they all shot into Black Forest...Needles mock-griping the entire time. Shaking my head and chuckling, I said goodbye to Mr. Pine and stepped inside Black Forest.

Which is like stepping into another world...at least, for me it is.

Taking a moment to enjoy the rush of physical and emotional strength that washed over me each and every time I stepped into Black Forest, I pushed off my hood and did what I always do... gave chase to Needles and the fireflies through the trees.

I knew Black Forest like I knew the back of my hand. Every twist and turn. I jumped over logs and called out hello to the age-old sentinels keeping watch—the pines, oaks, poplars, willows, redwoods, and countless other trees growing inside Black Forest. Even the woodland creatures were eager to play despite the rainy, cool night.

It didn't take long before I reached the clearing. The place where my dad stood guard. Dad was a Genius Loci. That meant he was literally the heart and soul of Black Forest. The protector of the trees and animals within. As the largest tree in Black Forest, he'd stood guard over Enchanted Island for thousands of years.

He was magnificent.

He was imposing.

He was my dad.

I waved and called out a greeting as I sprinted toward him.

When I was younger, I'd jump up onto his giant roots and run the length of him...but those days are few and far between. Now, I preferred to levitate myself and save my back and legs. Landing at the base of his trunk, I threw my arms around him as far as they would go and rested my cheek against his rough bark. This was a ritual that never grew old.

"Daughter of my Heart," Dad whispered. *"It is good to see you tonight. You did not have to make the journey in this wet weather."*

"Nonsense." I stepped back and turned before sitting, resting my back against his trunk. "Of course Needles and I would come see you."

"Your mother was here just before supper. She said there is much destruction on the island. Downed trees, mudslides, and even some roads washed away."

"Yes, and with a hurricane blowing in tomorrow, I assume it will get worse before it gets better."

"I have some of the animals checking on the north side of the island. I want to make sure our friends there are safe."

"Thanks, Dad. I would venture that way tomorrow, but Tommy Trollman discovered a body today, and I'm taking the lead."

"Another murder?" Dad mused.

"Afraid so. Someone kill an elderly troll named Eldon Stonebridge. He had a cute trinket shop set back in the woods. Sort of an out-of-the-way place. He didn't want to leave it to his only living heir, so he made a deal with Tommy." I raised my head and marveled at the joy of looking up and not being drenched by water. Dad was so huge, his many branches and leaves protected me from the rain. "I think the old troll was trying to play matchmaker as well."

Dad chuckled. *"With Tommy?"*

"Yep. I see it, and Tommy sees it…but I'm not sure if the woman does yet or not. She has two small children, and she's running, Dad. She told me today her husband was not a nice man. He was angry when it became apparent his son was a normal, but when the little girl showed promising magical abilities as a newborn, the man's anger grew violent."

"Then it was smart for her to flee here. That is what Enchanted Island is all about. Comforting those who need comfort. Imagine if I would have turned my back on your ancestors when they cried out to me those four-hundred-plus years ago?"

"I basically told her that. She could hide here, and we would keep her secret."

"How old is the little girl?"

I laughed. "Like two. And, Dad, she's something. Maybe not as powerful as the twins, but she'll be strong, like Jayden Sparks. Zac's little girl is quite skilled for only being three."

"I have huge concerns, Black Forest King," Needles said as he drifted out of Dad's branches to land on my shoulder. *"Huge concerns."*

"And what would those concerns be, old friend?" Dad asked.

"The twins are like nothing I've ever encountered before, Black Forest King. And Jayden and this little girl I met today are powerful for ones so young, and then you bring in all those Mystic kids." He sighed, his wings glowing blue and red. *"I worry the island may explode before they all get out of puberty."*

Dad and I laughed.

"He may not be wrong," I said. "I sometimes forget how… creative and rambunctious those Mystic kids are."

"They are terrors!" Needles cried. *"Do you forget the time they dropped their baby sister out of the tree just to see if she could fly? She was a baby, Princess!"*

I laughed even harder. "I do not forget, Needles. Nor do I forget all the other times they've about given me a heart attack."

"*I see great things for the generation behind Zoie Stone,*" Dad said. "*Great things, indeed. Do not worry, old friend. Enchanted Island will survive. Now, tell me more about this murder.*"

And so I did. I told him about Tommy discovering the body, about Pepper and her children hiding in the woods, and about the suspects I had so far. I'd just finished talking when Dad sighed.

"*Alex Stone is flying in. Our time has come to an end, Daughter of my Heart. Stay warm and safe tonight.*"

"We will. I'll check in again when I can. Between the investigation and the hurricane, my time tomorrow will be limited. But Alex, Grant, Walt, and Deputy Sparks are doing everything they can to make sure all the citizens on Enchanted Island are safe during the storm. Plus, I know Mom, GiGi, and a group from their coven, and a couple fairies are all staying on the eastern side of the island since that's where the eye of the storm is supposed to hit. Hopefully, they can direct the storm away from land."

"*I have no doubt everyone will do their best. Needles, watch over my daughter, please.*"

Needles leaped from my shoulder, his wings glowing gold and silver as Alex landed softly a few feet away. "*With my life, Black Forest King. With my life.*"

16

"I think we should stakeout Parker Stonebridge first," I shouted over the driving wind and rain. "Then maybe, if we're not miserable and wet enough afterward, we can either spy on Barton Longtree, Vera Wingsom, or Linus Gallion. All were out and about in town early in the morning and have no one to verify when they returned home. So all of them had opportunity as far as I'm concerned. Of course, Linus lives in an apartment, so a stakeout there might be a little harder."

"It shouldn't be but another five minutes," Alex's deep voice called out. When he was in his gargoyle form, his voice always deepened an octave or two. "Try to stay warm."

I buried my covered head in his chest and closed my eyes. Outside of freezing rain and snow, Alex's stone exterior could usually tolerate any form of weather. It was only when the rain or snow threatened to freeze his wings did he have to worry about flying in bad weather.

When I felt us starting to descend, I lifted my head and gazed out around me. Between the rain and the darkness, it was difficult to see...but I could just make out the carriage house behind Gloria Stonebridge's house. The minute Alex's feet touched the ground, I jumped out of his arms and released Needles from my pocket as Alex shifted back to his human form. Lifting one side of my hood, I waited for Needles to settle down inside before turning to my husband.

"I see why Gloria couldn't say for sure whether or not her son was home this morning. Those tall clusters of arborvitae shrubs make it impossible to see between the two houses."

"There are lights on inside the carriage house," Alex said. "Hopefully, that means Parker is inside."

The sky lit up with a spiderweb of lightning. Five seconds later, a giant rumble of thunder followed.

"Another storm rolling in," Alex said. "Let's hurry and see what Parker is up to."

We jogged to the front of the carriage house. The first floor was a garage, with the living quarters on the second floor. I was about to levitate myself up to the second floor when I heard arguing.

Alex put his finger to his lips, then motioned for me to follow him. With our backs pressed against the outside of the garage, I held my breath as the sound of the garage door opened. It wouldn't take much for us to be discovered.

"This is dumb, Ma!" Parker yelled. "Why do I have to do this tonight?"

"Because I said so. Now, go take care of this. Whatever it takes. You hear me, Parker? Whatever it takes!"

"Stone! How many times do I have to tell you to call me Stone? Dang! Show me some respect!"

"I'll show you respect when you get this done." Gloria's voice sounded even closer now. "I mean it. Don't come back to this house until it's taken care of."

A few seconds later, a figure strode out of the garage and headed toward the main house. I couldn't be positive because the face was hidden, but I was pretty sure it was Gloria Stonebridge. Had she turned back to look at her son…she'd have seen us pressed against the outside of the garage.

"Want me to see what's going on?" Needles mused.

"Let's wait a few more seconds," Alex whispered.

There was some muttering and cursing and a couple items being thrown around, but then I heard the sound of a car door being slammed shut. Alex grabbed my hand and yanked me down behind one of the bushes near the carriage house. Once again, lightning split the sky, and I held my breath, hoping we wouldn't be discovered.

Seconds later, headlights shown over the tops of our heads, and then as Parker turned his car around, we watched his taillights get smaller as he drove off.

"He's gone," Alex said, standing and tugging me up. "What do you want to do? Follow him or—"

He broke off when the sky opened and the rain came down even harder. I winced as the raindrops beat against my covered head. No matter how badly I wanted to continue following Parker, I knew it wasn't safe.

"This is ridiculous!" I shouted. "We aren't going to get anywhere tonight with this rain. I hate to say this, but I think we need to call it a night."

Alex gazed after the fading taillights. "I didn't like the sound of the argument. Where do you suppose Parker is going?"

I shook my head. "No idea. Maybe the store or Eldon's cottage? Do you want to try to—" The wind picked up again, and a row of shingles flew off the roof of the carriage house. "Yeah. I think we're done here. Will you be able to get us back home safely?"

"I should have stayed inside Black Forest."

"I'll get us home," Alex said. "I'm sorry we won't be able to stop by and see Tommy."

"Poor Tommy! I hope he stays safe."

Alex shifted into his gargoyle form and carefully swept me up into his arms. "I'm sure he'll be fine. I can't say as much for wherever Parker went."

"Maybe he went to go find a better nickname," Needles joked.

As Alex took to the sky, I rested my head against his chest and thought about the argument between Parker and Gloria. Where was she sending Parker to in such a terrible storm? And what did she mean when she said Parker had better take care of it? What "it" was she talking about?

17

"Grant just texted," Alex said early the next morning as we stood in the kitchen sipping our coffee. "He's following Serena and the twins to the bakery before grabbing a box of goodies. I guess that means Serena decided to open the bakery today."

"Thank goodness," Needle said, shoving a pretzel rod in his mouth. *"I was afraid I might starve."*

The storm had let up around three in the morning, and according to the supernatural weatherman a moment ago, the tropical storm that was upgraded to a Category One hurricane could come a little earlier than previously thought.

"Yeah," I said. "On our girls' group chat, Tamara said she'd go in around five and start the cinnamon rolls and sourdough bread. They'll do a limited selection today."

"This might make your day," Alex said as he finished the last of his coffee. "I told Opal and Pearl they didn't have to come in. All emergency calls will be routed to my cell phone."

I laughed. "That means Pearl can't give me a hard time this morning before we go back to Doc's lab."

"More like you can't give Pearl a hard time," Alex said before leaning down and kissing my cheek. "C'mon. We should go."

Since we were both going to be busy balancing the murder investigation and the impending storm, Alex and I decided to drive separately. Even with the continual rain and two stops for roadside help, we were able to pull in front of the station in relatively good time.

"I need to send Walt a quick text telling him about the call I just got," Alex said as he opened the front door for us. "He and your aunt are going to be helping out in town today."

"I'll wait for you in the sheriff's office. Since Opal's not there, someone will need to make sure thieves don't come by and steal all our pretzels."

Once the text was sent, Alex and I descended the stairs, bypassing the desk where Pearl usually sat harassing everyone who came in, and quickly made our way down the hallway. Doc's laboratory was the first door on the right.

Alex knocked once before pushing open the door. Finn, Doc, and Grant were already in the lab waiting for us.

"Morning," Finn chirped, taking a huge gulp of her coffee.

I smiled. "You're awfully chipper for someone who couldn't have had much sleep."

Finn nodded. "Well, this is my fifth cup of coffee, and Grant just gave me some of Serena's delicious sourdough bread for dinner tonight, so I'm in a pretty good mood."

"Your makeup is on point as well," I said.

Finn waved her hands in front of her face. "You like? I figured with all the rain and water coming in, blue would be the color for the day."

And it wasn't just the shimmery blue eyeshadow and blue stud earrings lining both ears, left nostril, and right eyebrow…it was also the blue dye she'd used to tip the spikes in her dark hair.

"Now that we're all here," Doc said. "Why don't we get started." He motioned us over to the body on the slab. "Eldon Stonebridge. Eighty-two-year-old troll. Cause of death was blunt force trauma to the head. Specifically, to the temple." He pointed to the gash on the side of Eldon's head. "The thing is, Eldon was not in good health. He had Swamp Whisper Syndrome, a disease that only trolls develop. I gave him maybe one to three months to live."

I nodded. "That's about what Tommy told us Eldon had told him."

"I put time of death between 9:30 and 10:00." Doc covered the top half of Eldon's body with a white sheet, and we all stepped back from the table.

"I actually have quite a bit of information for you," Finn said. "I finally got a match back on the partial print on the zipper pull I told you about last night. The partial print belongs to Parker Stonebridge. Unfortunately, the cauldron, which was the murder weapon, was too porous to get prints from. It did have blood splatter on it, but the blood came back as belonging to Eldon. Also, there were no prints on the label that belonged to Pepper Hollis. Probably whoever laid it on the counter used magic to levitate it off the ground. Sorry about that. I did find another set of fingerprints on a shattered snow globe. They came back belonging to Barton Longtree."

I blinked in surprise at that. "Really? Because he told us he'd never been to Eldon's store. And if Pepper comes in on Sunday nights to dust and sweep, then that means chances are high Barton was there sometime this week."

"I'm over halfway done with piecing everything together. I'll need about another four hours, I estimate. Oh, and I have the mold of the tire tread completed."

"That's great," I said. "With the amount of people at the store throughout the week and yesterday morning, it could be just a random tire tread, but every little thing helps. We have plenty of leads to go on, Finn. Thanks."

"The hurricane is supposed to hit the island around three or four," Doc said. "I have dragon shifter friends who will fly the sky to help the witches and fairies track the storm. Make sure you all take shelter. If I'm still here, I'll just stay in my lab. Underground like it is, it's a safe place to be."

Grant nodded. "We have a backup plan. Serena promised to be done at the bakery by 2:00, locked up and heading home with the twins. If she does happen to still be in town for some reason, or the storm comes early, then she's supposed to go to her mom's place."

"Sounds like we're all prepared," Doc said. "You know what that means?"

I smiled. "Nothing will go according to plan."

He nodded solemnly. "Exactly. Stay safe, everyone."

18

Back upstairs, I got the coffee around as Grant pulled out the bakery goodies and Alex got the chairs in order around Grant's desk. Needles was already chomping away on his caramel-dipped pretzel rod.

I set the coffees on the desk, and then grabbed the lemon-blueberry muffin. "Bless Tamara for getting a few muffins in this morning."

Grant smiled. "There weren't many. They sell way more cinnamon rolls than muffins, but I made sure to snag you a couple."

After eating half his large cinnamon roll, Grant set it down, took a drink of coffee, then wiped off his hands before picking up a stack of papers. "Got the backgrounds back from PADA. I'm going to start with Eldon's niece, Gloria Stonebridge. Age, forty-eight. Troll. Divorced, one adult son. She has lived on Enchanted Island for two years now, ever since her father died. According to the records I pulled from the courthouse, she inherited the house that once belonged to her father, George Stonebridge, who was Eldon's older brother. Gloria used to work as a rare book restorer, but as of right now, she's unemployed since moving to Enchanted Island. She has one ding on her criminal record. Twelve years ago, she was arrested in the supernatural courts for forgery. She served two weeks in jail, and then she had four years of probation. Her financials are in decent shape, but that's only after she inherited from her dad who died two years ago."

"Motive?" Alex asked.

"Two possible," I said. "She admitted she knew Eldon was sick, so maybe she was ready to inherit and decided to kill him. But I think there's a stronger motive in that she found out somehow Eldon had sold not only his store, but his two properties and acreage to Tommy Trollman. In a fit of anger, she and her son killed him."

"Alibi?" Alex asked.

"She claims she was at her house all morning until she arrived at Eldon's shop around 11:30 to speak with him. That's when she discovered he was dead. There is no one who can corroborate her statement."

"Next, we have Gloria's son, Parker 'Stone' Stonebridge. Age, twenty-two. Half troll, half fairy. Single, no children. You guys aren't going to believe this kid's criminal record already in his young life—it's pretty extensive. Juvie record is sealed, but if we feel it's needed, we can have PADA open it. Got out of juvie at eighteen, then got arrested for assault and battery and petty theft in the supernatural town of Haunted Falls. Did three years for that. Moved back to Enchanted Island last year when he got out."

I whistled. "This kid is heading down the wrong path if he doesn't change his ways soon."

Grant nodded. "Looks that way. As you can imagine, his

financials are a mess. Massive debt. I show no employment history."

Alex chuckled. "Unless you count the zipper pull business he's trying to establish."

"Stone zipper pulls," I said. "Which, interestingly enough, one was found at our crime scene. Parker told me he hadn't been to see Eldon at the store in about a month. I think the zipper pull being present negates that statement. We'll definitely want to talk with him about that."

"Alibi?" Alex mused.

"Almost identical to his mom's alibi. States he was at his house—it's a carriage house behind the main house. Only problem is because of a row of arborvitaes shrubs, you can't see the two houses. Parker says he was at home all morning until he saw his mom around 11:00. That's when they left together to go see Eldon at his shop."

"And why were they going to see him?" Grant asked.

"According to Gloria, Eldon called her and said he wanted to speak to her. About what she didn't know, but she admitted she knew he was sick. She made it sound like she was expecting to go there and have Eldon go over his will with her, or to tell her he was leaving her everything when he passes."

Grant took a sip of his coffee. "So your theory is maybe they met around 9:30, not 11:30, and that's when Eldon told them he signed over his holdings to Tommy Trollman. They got angry, and one or both of them killed Eldon?"

I nodded. "Yes. I like that theory a lot."

"Next up," Grant said, "is Barton Longtree. Age, eighty-three. Fairy. Divorced, three adult children. Two of his three children live off the island. Barton was born and raised on Enchanted Island. Criminal history is mostly misdemeanors for fighting and terroristic threats. Those also involved Eldon Stonebridge.

Barton also filed two civil cases against Eldon over the years, but nothing came of either one of them."

"Motive?" Alex asked.

"They are long-time rivals," I said. "Barton made no bones about the fact he still didn't like Eldon even after all these years. They went into business together when they were in their mid-twenties. A few years later, they would split due to—well, basically over ethics and how the business should be run. Barton said Eldon went so far as to accuse him of embezzlement. As evidenced by the numerous arrests and civil cases filed, these two men never saw eye-to-eye on anything." I took a sip of my coffee. "And it gets even weirder. Barton accused Eldon of cursing him."

"I have to admit, Shayla," Alex said, taking a drink of his coffee, "I'm thinking, why now? After all these years, why would Barton just up and kill Eldon?"

"I don't know. But I do know Barton lied. He told me the last time he saw Eldon, it was in town. He told me he'd never been to the shop before. Yet, Finn found Barton's fingerprints on a snow globe in the broken glass found at the crime scene. So Barton isn't telling us the truth. We'll need to speak to him again. Right now, I don't know of a better motive other than long-standing hatred, but we'll probably get one once we know when and why Barton journeyed out to Eldon's store."

"Alibi?" Alex mused.

"He drove into town around 7:30 to put a 'family emergency' sign on his shop so he could stay closed due to the storm. He saw his granddaughter in town around 8:15, and then he said he went straight home. No one at home to corroborate his statement."

"Let's go next with Barton's granddaughter, Ellie Longtree. Age, twenty-seven. Fairy. Born and raised on Enchanted Island. Has worked for Supernatural Insurance Underwriters for the past five years. I called them and they confirm she was logged in to her laptop at 9:00. They don't show her logging out until she took a lunch around 1:00. No criminal history, and her financials look decent."

"Motive?" Alex mused.

"Her grandfather was Eldon's business rival, *and* she's dating a vendor who sells at both Eldon's and Barton's stores. Does she have a motive? I'm not sure it's clear yet. Maybe she got mad Eldon was cutting her boyfriend's paycheck? But that doesn't seem to be reason enough to kill. So I'm keeping her in reserve. I'm not sure if there is a clear motive, yet."

"What about her alibi?" Alex asked.

"She was with Dalton Fowler. They went to breakfast at Enchanted Island Café. They were home by 9:00 so she could go to work. She worked until 1:00, then took a break for lunch. I saw them walking to Vera Wingsom's house during her lunch break."

"So then let's go with Dalton Fowler next," Grant said. "Age, thirty-five. Fairy. Single. Moved to Enchanted Island about six years ago. Criminal history consists of a misdemeanor charge of unauthorized spell casting some ten years ago in the supernatural town of Spellville. He and two friends were picked up on the side of the road and charged. He did community service and paid a fine. He has some outstanding debt. He's self-employed and makes his living selling his artwork around town. No social media presence or selling on the supernatural internet that I could find."

"Motive?" Alex asked.

"Eldon changed his contract with Dalton. Instead of Dalton getting seventy percent of the money from the sale of his items, he was now getting sixty percent. When he confronted Eldon about it, Eldon told him he could take it or leave it. Dalton also admitted Eldon knew he was selling to other stores on the island, including Barton Longtree's store. Dalton claims to have no beef with Eldon, but I could tell from the tic in his cheek he wasn't happy about the change in the contract. Especially when he intimated not *all* vendors were being cut in profits. When I pressed more, he said he doubted the woman who makes the jellies and baskets was being cut. The way he said it made me think he thought maybe something untoward was going on between Eldon and Pepper Hollis."

"*Was* there anything untoward?" Alex asked.

I snorted. "No. Like I said, I think Eldon Stonebridge had something else in mind when it came to Pepper. He seemed to care for her, and she obviously cared for him. She went on and on about how he took her in and gave her and her children a place to live."

"So what's the something else?" Grant asked.

I smiled. "I think Eldon was trying to play matchmaker. In his own time, of course. It's obvious Pepper is healing from some wounds, but I think Eldon wanted to match up Pepper and Tommy Trollman."

Grant's mouth dropped. "Seriously? Do they know?"

"*Tommy does,*" Needles said, his wings glowing red and pink. "*And I don't think he minds at all.*"

"Interesting," Grant murmured.

"It definitely should be fun to watch," Alex agreed.

I nodded and couldn't help the grin that spread across my face. "Yeah. It should be *very* interesting."

"So Dalton's alibi?" Alex asked.

"He was with Ellie Longtree. They went to breakfast and returned home by 9:00 for her to start work. He said he worked on new creations in his shed. He didn't come back inside the house until Ellie took a break for a late lunch, and then he and

Ellie walked over to Vera's house afterward so he could check on her. I guess he does that a lot for Vera—checks up on her and makes sure she's doing okay."

"Next is Vera Wingsom." Grant reached over and snatched an oatmeal cookie out of the bakery box. "Age, seventy-one. Fairy. Widowed, one adult son living off the island. Vera has lived on Enchanted Island her entire life. No criminal record, and no major outstanding debt."

"Motive?" Alex asked.

"She's been in love with Eldon for over fifty years," I said. "The story from Barton Longtree is Eldon came to Vera's grandmother when Vera was not quite an adult and asked for a curse to give to Barton Longtree. Vera fell in love right then and there. When questioning Vera, she tried to downplay her feelings at first, but Needles and I saw through it. She cried when we told her about his dying, and even Dalton Fowler, her neighbor, asked her about her feelings toward Eldon. Like it was news to him. And it probably was. She was good at keeping her cards close to her vest, it seems."

"So the motive is some kind of unrequited love?" Alex mused. "After all this time?"

Grant shrugged. "Maybe Vera knew he was dying, and she got mad he'd rather die alone than with her?"

"I like that theory," Needles said. *"You don't love me, then you won't ever love anyone."*

"Plus," I added, "she knew about Pepper living in Eldon's extra cottage and she has kids. Could be she said enough was enough."

Alex nodded. "Okay. And her alibi?"

I finished off the last of my lemon-blueberry muffin before responding. "She ran to Enchanted Bakery & Brew around 8:00 and was there for about an hour. Serena and Tamara have both confirmed this. She claims she was home by 9:15. No one to verify."

"Before I get to the last person," Grant said, "can I ask why you texted last night and called off the background check on Pepper Hollis?"

"I'm almost one hundred percent sure you won't find anything under that name," I said. "And I don't want to raise any red flags. Pepper told me she was running from an abusive ex-husband who is a prominent member of his town. I got the feeling maybe the mayor, or judge, or cop, or something like that because the fear was real when she implied if I ran a check, he'd know. So I took that into consideration, and I'm trusting my gut. She didn't kill Eldon. And she sure as heck wouldn't take her kids there to the store to see it. I found them hiding in a log, fleeing from the killer. I pretty much know everything I need to know already. She's a hardworking fairy who has fled from an abusive situation. She has a normal son and a daughter who shows remarkable magical power."

"I'd like to know who the ex-husband is," Alex growled.

"On that we agree, Gargoyle," Needles grumbled. *"I'd take my time inflicting pain on the man."*

"Now I understand," Grant said. "Okay, the last person I have a background for is Linus Gallion. Age, thirty-seven. Witch. Single. He moved to Enchanted Island eight years ago. Works from home as a data analyst for Enchanted Analytics. No criminal history. Financially secure, but I show a lot of money being spent on gamer programs and collectibles." He looked up and grinned. "I think I'd like to see this guy's place."

I shuttered. "No, you wouldn't. It was…odd."

Grant grinned. "Did he have a life-size cardboard cutout of Princess Leia in the living room?"

My mouth dropped. "How did you know?"

Grant and Alex both chuckled and high-fived each other.

"Motive?" Alex asked.

"This guy is *serious* about his collections and about collectors in general. He was livid Eldon would have such an outstanding collection and not let anyone near it. Linus told me Eldon didn't deserve what he had. There was something…I don't know. Maybe I don't get people like this, but it just seemed too weird for me. His cat was named after Ms. Pac-Man. He had all kinds of movie and comic and gaming memorabilia around his apartment. Even his furniture pieces and fixtures were collectibles."

"Serious collectors will do anything for just the right piece," Grant said. "I worked with another cop years ago, a human. He was intense. The man could quote movie stats, could rhapsodize over different conspiracies regarding certain movie comic franchises. And he had quite the collection at his house." He grinned. "Single guy who thought nothing of spending a couple thousand on just the right action figure."

"I wonder if I can make me into an action figure?" Needles mused. *"I bet I'd go for a lot of money."*

"So where does this leave you?" Alex mused, ignoring Needles' wild assertions. "What's your next step?"

A huge clap of thunder shook the windows, and I stood to refill my coffee cup. "I need to question Parker Stonebridge about the zipper pull being at the store, and I want to find out where he went last night. Something about that whole thing didn't sit right. I then need to talk to Barton Longtree about why his fingerprints were on a snow globe in Eldon's shop. After that, I'm just going to press my suspects a little more. Shake the tree until something falls."

"Need help?" Alex's cell phone rang, and he grimaced. "It's the dispatch line." He slid his finger over the icon and answered.

A few minutes later, he was standing and motioning for Grant as he disconnected. "Vehicle in water over off Spellbound Street. I'm going to fly over and take a look. Can you follow in your car?"

"You got it," Grant said, already jogging toward the door.

"Sorry, Shayla." Alex leaned over and kissed my cheek. "We'll catch up later. Promise. Be safe."

"You too. I'll lock up when I leave."

Needles flew to my shoulder. *"We better get started, Princess. Something tells me it could be a long day today."*

The loud boom from another round of thunder seemed to punctuate Needles' thoughts perfectly.

19

Barton Longtree opened his door and scowled. "Now what? I answered all your questions yesterday."

"You answered them," I said. "You just didn't answer them truthfully. So now we're going to try it again."

"What are you talking about?"

"You told me yesterday you never visited Eldon Stonebridge's shop, Across the Bridge Trinkets. Do you remember that?"

"Of course I remember saying that. It's true."

"Then how did your fingerprints get on a snow globe that was in Eldon's shop?"

The look of surprise that crossed Barton's face was almost comical. "How do you know about that?"

"That's the thing about forensic evidence, Barton. It doesn't lie. Your fingerprints were found at the scene of the crime, and I am simply wondering how that could be if you'd never stepped foot in that shop?"

"Okay, fine. So maybe I was in there yesterday morning."

When he didn't say anything, I pressed a little harder. "Why were you there?"

"Because that fool sent me a letter in the mail Wednesday telling me he was dying and didn't have long to live. He said he'd like to see me Thursday morning before the store opened. He told me to be there around 8:30. I thought maybe he was going to apologize for being a horrible friend all these years and for cursing me...but no. I get there, and he brags how he'd secured someone to take over his store and make sure it lived on long after he was dead. And if things went the way he hoped, the new owner would crush me and my business. I demanded to know who he'd sold to, and he said he could probably tell me since people would know soon enough." He curled his lip. "Tommy Trollman."

"Why is that bad for you?"

"Tommy and I have...well, we'll call it a 'dislike' for each other. That old troll knew he'd be getting the last laugh by selling to Tommy. So I got mad, picked up the closest thing, and threw it across the store before storming out. I guess it was a snow globe. I wasn't even paying attention. That's how mad I was."

"You expect us to believe that? You got mad, you threw something, and then walked right out the door without a backward glance?"

"It's what happened, I tell you!"

"Five minutes alone with him, and I bet I could get him to tell the truth."

I crossed my arms over my chest. "I'm sure I don't have to tell you that it doesn't look good for you to lie to the police."

"I ain't lying! When I left Eldon's store around 8:45, that old troll was still alive. Why are you hounding me, anyway? Did you look at Vera Wingsom? She's not right when it comes to Eldon. My granddaughter, Ellie, told me she has a room in her cottage dedicated to all things Eldon! I'm telling you, she's your killer."

"That's all we have for right now. If we have any more questions, we'll probably be doing a formal interview down at the sheriff's station. Just so you know, Mr. Longtree."

"Yeah, yeah, yeah."

He shut the door in my face.

Flipping the hood up on my raincoat, I dashed to my Bronco. Opening the door, Needles zipped in ahead of me. When he got to the passenger seat, he shook his quills, spraying water everywhere.

"Was that really necessary?"

He grinned, snatched up a pretzel from the backpack, and flew to the backseat. *"It was totally necessary, Princess."*

I pulled out of Barton's driveway and made a right at the end of the road. "I was going to go see Parker Stonebridge next, but let's stop by Vera's house and see if we can't get a peek at this shrine room she has of Eldon. Then we'll go talk to Parker."

"This Vera lady really had it bad for Eldon."

"What bothers me more, Needles, is the fact Ellie knew about the love room but kept it a secret. If we believe Dalton didn't know the extent of Vera's feelings, then why would Ellie see the room and not mention it to him…but she mentions it to her grandfather? Why?"

"Maybe Barton and Ellie want to throw suspicion onto Vera? They know about the love room, and so they casually mention it when it looks like we're getting close to naming Barton as the killer?"

"Maybe."

I traversed the streets slowly and carefully, taking extra care when crossing the roads with standing water. When I finally reached Vera's cottage, I breathed a sigh of relief. Getting out of the Bronco and tucking Needles inside my hood, I hurried up her walkway to her front door.

I was about to lift my hand and knock when the door swung open. "Oh, dear. Look at you, all wet. Come in. Come in. Do you need something warm to drink?"

"I'd love that, Ms. Wingsom." I stepped inside her living room, and Needles flew out from my hood. I made a point to stand on the towel she had on the floor, and using my magic, I suspended my raincoat above the towel to drip dry. "But before I have a drink, could I use your restroom?"

Vera blinked in surprise, looking down the hallway. "Oh, yes. Of course. It's the first door on the left. I'll go make us some hot tea, if that's okay with you?"

I smiled and nodded. "That sounds great."

As Vera and Needles headed toward the back of the house, I made a right and padded down the hallway. There was one door on the left, one door on the right, and one straight ahead at the end of the hallway. Figuring the one straight ahead would be the master bedroom, I looked behind me before opening the door on the right.

Shrine didn't do it justice. This was an entire room dedicated to all things Eldon Stonebridge. The walls were covered with pictures of Eldon at all stages of life—from mid-twenties until just a few months before he died, if I had to guess. There was even a cardboard cutout of him standing in the corner. It was well and truly creepy.

Hearing voices, I quickly shut the door and ducked into the bathroom. Turning on the water, I heard a knock on the door.

"Are you okay in there?" Vera asked.

"I'm fine, Ms. Wingsom. I'm afraid I'll need to take a raincheck on the tea." I dried my hands and opened the door, smiling out at the older woman. "I just got a call from dispatch.

There's been an emergency, and Alex and Grant are busy. I'm sorry."

Vera frowned. "Of course. But why did you stop by?"

"Oh, I wanted to ask you a couple more questions about Eldon and what you might have observed when you were at his shop. But that can wait. I really need to get this emergency."

Vera stepped back, and I hurried past her down the hallway. I had no idea if she believed me or not. Needles was hovering at the end of the hallway, his wings glowing purple and red.

"I take it you saw it? Was it creepy?"

Biting back a smile, I slipped on my raincoat and turned to face Vera. "Thanks again for the use of your bathroom." I opened the front door and Needles slipped inside my hood. "Stay inside where it's warm, okay?"

"Of course, dear. Only a foolish person would be out in this storm."

This time I did grin. Was she saying she thought I was foolish? I pulled the door closed and dashed to my Bronco. Hopping inside, I turned over the engine and buckled my seatbelt.

"Vera Wingsom had a very unhealthy attachment to Eldon," I said, pulling out of the driveway. "I just wish I had more time to look around. Maybe find a clue. Next stop, Parker Stonebridge's place."

20

Fifteen minutes later, I pulled into Gloria Stonebridge's long driveway. The ride through town had opened my eyes to just how much rain we'd truly had overnight. I had to cross Spellbound Street, so I saw where Alex and Grant had been called out to. Weston's Auto was also on site, the tow truck pulling out a submerged car. A weeping vampire, who looked no more than twenty, was crying on the side of the road as she spoke to Alex and Grant.

I was about to bypass the main house and head for the carriage house around back, when I saw two figures in the front window arguing. Pulling the Bronco to a stop, I got out and hurried to the front door, Needles hovering next to my shoulder.

I rang the doorbell and waited. The rain had let up just a little, but I was still bone-chillingly cold. It didn't take long before Gloria Stonebridge opened the door. She was dressed casually in black pants and a gray sweater, and her hair was pulled back from her face.

"Agent Loci-Stone. What brings you out on such a dreary day?"

"I need to speak to your son. I saw him in the window."

Gloria sighed. "I suppose you should come in out of the rain. I'll ask you stay in the foyer, though. I don't want water dripped all over my house. You understand?"

"Nope. Sure don't. What are you hiding?"

"Of course," I said, ignoring Needles.

I stepped inside and stood on the mat, letting the water pool at my feet. Gloria took two steps backward and looked over her right shoulder. "Parker, you need to come in here immediately. Someone needs to speak with you."

Gloria looked down at my feet and sighed. I was about to tell her I could clean it up with some magic if she wanted, but Parker came jogging into the foyer. He stopped in his tracks when he saw me, and his face lost all color.

"You need to speak to me?" Parker squeaked. "Why?"

"You told me yesterday you had not been to Eldon's store in over a month. Is that correct?"

Parker shot his mom a look before answering. "That's right."

I pulled out my phone and brought up the evidence bag with his zipper pull inside. "Can you identify this for me?"

Parker looked down at my phone and gulped. "That's one of mine."

I took back my phone. "Can you tell me how it appeared at the crime scene if you hadn't been inside Across the Bridge Trinkets in over a month?"

Again, Parker shot his mom a look. "Okay, maybe I was there a couple days ago."

"What?" Gloria demanded.

I held up my hand to stop her. "Please be more specific, Parker. What day and what time were you there?"

"Wednesday afternoon. I wanted Eldon to sell my zipper pulls in his store. The guy's family, after all. He should do that for me."

"Why would you do that?" Gloria demanded. "He'd already told you no."

"Because he's family, and I figured he'd want in on the ground floor. You know, be there when it all happened. These things are gonna go big. I just know it."

"And what did Eldon say?" I asked.

Parker scowled. "He laughed and said he'd rather have a meal with Barton Longtree than sell my zipper pulls in his store."

Needles laughed, and his wings turned purple and green. *"That was a good one."*

"And this was Wednesday afternoon?" I asked.

"Yes."

"One last question. Where did you go last night between the hours of 8:00 and 10:00?"

Parker's mouth dropped, and even Gloria looked shocked. Parker turned to his mom and held up one hand, as though imploring her to say something. When it became obvious she wasn't going to say anything, he narrowed his eyes at her, and a flush crept up his neck.

"I ran an errand for my mom."

"Don't you drag me into this," Gloria hissed.

I thought that was telling, since Gloria had told Parker he couldn't return home until he had completed what it was she requested. And now she was going to leave him twisting in the wind.

"Mom wanted me to go out to the store and see if I could break in. She wanted those collectibles in the cabinet."

"Shut up," Gloria hissed.

I narrowed my eyes at her. "Ma'am, if you don't keep quiet, I can make it so that all of us go down to the station, and we have a formal interview."

Gloria folded her arms across her chest and glared...but she didn't argue.

"I called this guy I know," Parker continued, "and I told him if he helped me break in, I would let him have one of whatever collectible inside the cabinet he wanted. He said he'd be there at 8:00."

"I personally warded that store," I said. "There's no way you got in."

Parker's face turned red, and he stared down at the ground. "Yeah, me and Linus tried for like an hour, but we couldn't get in."

"Linus?" I mused. "I assume you mean Linus Gallion?"

"Yeah. I knew he'd jump at the chance for one of the collectables."

"Then what happened after you couldn't get into the store last night?"

"We left. He drove off, and I went home. I stopped by the house and told mom I couldn't get inside the store. She was pretty ticked."

I shook my head. "You realize I can have you arrested for trying to break in, correct?"

Parker shrugged. "I guess. It's not like we actually got in and stole anything."

"Is he really that dumb?" Needles demanded. *"Never mind. I remember his rap sheet."*

I folded my arms across my chest and stared at Gloria and then at Parker. "I ran your criminal record, Parker. I know you've pretty much been in trouble your entire life. Juvie, then jail. You go back to jail, and you'll be staying a long time. Do you understand that, Parker?"

Parker did his best to feign disinterest, but I saw the anger lurking underneath. "Of course I understand. Why do you think I didn't want to go last night? But Eldon had already yanked back our inheritance. We deserved something for looking after that old guy for the last two years."

"Maybe your mother looked after him, but I know for a fact you just got out of jail less than a year ago. And you and your mom were *never* guaranteed an inheritance. You need to rethink these bad decisions you're making. I can promise you, you do one thing wrong on Enchanted Island, and you will have more than me to answer to. Sheriff Stone and Detective Wolfe are aware of your past. If you want your past to stay in the past, then you need to make smarter decisions from here on out."

"If that's all," Gloria said stiffly, "then I will thank you to leave my property."

"I mean it, Gloria. He makes one bad step, and he'll be going away for a long time. I'll be in touch if I have more questions."

21

"Let's go see Linus Gallion real quick," I said to Needles as I pulled out of the Stonebridge's driveway. "Then maybe stop by Across the Bridge Trinkets to make sure everything looks good there, and then pop in on Pepper and the kids. I want to make sure Devona was able to stop by."

We drove in silence to Linus' house. The rain had picked up once again, and it took all my concentration to stay on the road. According to my phone app, the winds were at 60 mph. Add the driving rain on top of it, and it was all I could do to keep the Bronco on the road.

I parked in the guest parking at the apartment complex, and Needles and I headed upstairs to Linus Gallion's apartment. I knocked on the door, but when no one answered, I knocked again. Placing my ear against the door, I tried to hear if there was a TV on.

"Maybe he went out," Needles said.

"Maybe. But I think I hear the TV."

I knocked again.

Nothing.

Reaching down, I turned the knob...and was shocked when the door swung open. Linus must have been attacked when he opened the door because his body lay crumpled on the ground just a couple feet from where I stood.

"*Can you tell what killed him?*" Needles asked.

"Not yet. Try to find Ms. P, would you?"

"*Sure thing, Princess.*"

I called Doc and informed him about Linus and gave him the address. He assured me he and Finn would arrive shortly. I placed one more call to Alex, and then slipped the phone back inside my pocket. Kneeling down, I examined the body as much as I could without disturbing it. There was a small hole in the front of Linus' shirt, as though he'd been hit with a wave of magic and it had burned through. Like Eldon, there was an open gash on the side of Linus' temple.

Standing, I looked around for Needles.

"Needles? You find anything?"

Needles zipped back into the room from the hallway.

"*I found Ms. P. She's understandably distraught. She said there was a knock at the door last night, and Linus was playing his game on the TV. She saw him get up from the chair and open the door. He was in the way so she couldn't see, but she heard him cry out and fall to the ground. There was more noise, and she became frightened, and so she bolted from the room. She's still hiding under the bed, Princess. She won't come out.*"

"I'll think of something," I promised.

On one of the big screen TVs, the character in the role-playing game Linus had been playing was on the screen and motionless—much like the man on the floor—but I could still hear noises from the game.

Within fifteen minutes, Doc, Finn, Alex, and Grant strode through the front door of Linus's apartment. Each one was soaking wet and shivering.

As Finn and Grant recorded the scene, and Doc examined the body, Alex, Needles, and I went to knock on the neighbors' doors. There were four apartments in the upstairs hallway, one of them being Linus' apartment. That meant we had three potential witnesses.

Two residents didn't answer. I figured they were at work. But we got lucky on the third try. A female werewolf in her mid-fifties answered the door. She didn't look happy to see us.

"Hello, my name is Agent Loci-Stone, and these are my partners, Sheriff Stone and Needles. May we ask you a few questions?"

The woman sighed. "Do I have a choice?"

I forced a smile. "No. We need to ask you about your neighbor, Linus Gallion."

"Loner. Keeps to himself. What? Did he go on a mass shooting spree and kill fifty people? I wouldn't be surprised. You see those people on TV who are so shocked when their quiet, unassuming neighbor does something crazy like bury twenty bodies in the backyard. Not me. I totally expect that from Linus. He's weird."

"Good to know," I said. "Can you tell me the last time you saw Linus Gallion?"

"I don't know. It's been a couple of days. Like I said, the dude's odd. Keeps to himself. Never says hi when I say hi."

"Did you see him last night?" I asked. "Or did you hear anything from his apartment last night?"

"Lady, I hear weird stuff coming from his apartment all the time. He just sits in there and plays video games or watches science fiction stuff. There's always something strange coming from his apartment."

"So you didn't see him last night?" Alex asked.

The woman shook her head. "Nope. I haven't seen him in at least two days. Sorry, I can't help. If he's gone missing, I wouldn't worry. He's probably at a Star Trek convention or something." She took a step back and closed the door.

"Well, she was helpful," Needles snickered.

We retreated back to Linus' apartment, but before we entered, I put my hand on Alex's arm. "I spoke to Parker Stonebridge before we came here. He told me he and Linus went out to Eldon's store last night to break in and steal the memorabilia. I think it's time we bring in Parker and sweat him. Maybe he did this, maybe he didn't. But all signs are pointing to him."

Alex nodded. "Let's help Grant and Finn process the scene, and then he and I will go pick up Parker for you. Does that work for you?"

I smiled. "Works for me."

As we entered Linus' apartment, Finn motioned us over. "I found this in his hand." She held out an onyx zipper pull in her gloved hand. "I thought this might seal the deal for you."

I nodded. "Not only did Parker Stonebridge admit to trying to break into Eldon's shop with Linus last night, but now we find one of his zipper pulls in our dead guy's hand. Yeah, we need to bring Parker in."

Alex and I helped Grant and Finn process the scene while Doc finished examining the body. Thirty minutes later, everyone was finished and Finn and I were levitating Linus' body out the front door. The manager had come out to see what the commotion was about, but I let Grant handle that.

"Meet you at the station after we pick up Parker," Alex said.

"Needles and I will be there," I promised. "But first, I need to make a quick stop."

He gestured to Ms. P in the Death Star carrier. "Does it have something to do with the cat?"

I nodded. "Sure does."

22

"I don't know how many times I have to tell you," Parker said. "I don't know how the guy died. When he left the store last night, he was alive. I don't know how he died!"

Alex, Grant, Needles, and I were squeezed into the interview room with a terrified Parker Stonebridge. He was pale, clammy, and his eyes were continually darting around the room, not focusing on anyone. I was pretty sure I wasn't the only one who could smell his fear.

After leaving Linus' apartment, I'd driven out to Pepper Hollis' cottage to see if she might want to adopt Ms. P. When I arrived, Devona had been about to leave, so I spent a few minutes catching up with her while Jacob and Mia coaxed Ms. P out of the Death Star carrier. By the time I left, Ms. P seemed to be adjusting to her new place.

Leaning over the table, I peered into Parker's face. "What was the last thing your mom said to you last night? You know, before you left to meet Linus at the store? What did she say to you?"

Parker's eyes went wide. "You already know what she said!"

"Answer her question," Alex said. "What did your mother say to you?"

"She told me to do whatever it takes to get it done, and to not come back until I had. But she didn't mean—"

"She told you to do whatever it takes," I interrupted. "Did that mean kill Linus Gallion if things went south? Could you really trust him to keep his mouth shut? How well did you know him?"

"I only knew him because he sometimes dropped by the store when I was there," Parker whined. "And I liked the fact he gave my uncle such a hard time." He shrugged. "It was kinda cool. That's it. I didn't know him that well."

I leaned forward. "So it never crossed your mind that maybe he might try to come back on his own to steal the collectibles? That maybe you should make sure he *didn't* try that?"

Parker dropped his eyes and shifted in his chair. "Nah. Of course not."

Alex motioned toward the door with his eyes. Standing, Alex, Grant, and I moved toward the door, leaving a scared Parker at the table.

"I'll stay in here with the vicious killer, Princess," Needles said, his wings glowing red and orange.

"What about me?" Parker demanded. "When can I go? You can't keep me here forever!"

I turned and looked at him. "Not forever. But we *can* keep you for a while. Make yourself at home, Parker. You aren't going anywhere, anytime soon."

"Oh, c'mon man!" Parker cried. "This is ridiculous!"

I shut the door on his shouts.

"Was he at home or his mom's when you found him?" I asked.

"At his place," Alex said.

"Does Mom know we've detained him?" I asked.

Alex and Grant looked at each other and shrugged. "If she doesn't, I'm sure she will shortly."

I nodded. "Okay. Finn is still working on piecing all the broken glass together. Linus' murder sidetracked her a little. Hopefully, she'll come across another clue for us."

"Until then," Alex said, "what do you want to do with Parker?"

"We definitely have enough to detain him," I said. "He has admitted to being with Linus last night. He's admitted to attempted breaking and entering, and we've found his signature zipper pull in the hand of our latest victim. That's enough to keep him until Finn gives us something more, or until we find a smoking gun."

Grant smiled. "Or until he loses his mind and confesses."

I grinned. "Why do you think I left Needles in there?"

Both men laughed.

I glanced at my watch. "It's almost 3:00."

"Doc texted me while we were in the interview room," Alex said. "He figured he'd be just as safe in his lab as he would be at home, so he's going ahead with the autopsy now."

As if on cue, a loud boom filled the hallway, and the windows in the main room rattled.

"I think I'll check on Serena and the twins," Grant said. "She's supposed to be leaving shortly to go home."

"GiGi, Mom, and a bunch of the other coven witches and fairies are all on the east side of the island," I said. "They're supposed to be using magic to help push the eye of the storm away from the island. They can't stop the storm, of course. But they can try to keep the eye from moving across the entire island

and maybe just localize it around the eastern side, since it's coming up from the south."

Grant frowned. "Maybe I should have Serena stay in town? What do you guys think?"

"I think—"

I was cut off by the sound of the station's front door opening and Gloria Stonebridge's shrill voice filling the front room. "I demand to see my son!"

"Let's go," Alex said.

The three of us hurried down the hallway and rounded the corner to where Gloria stood near Opal's empty desk. She looked wild—her hair standing on end, her lips pinched, and she was panting. "Where is he?"

"He's being held for questioning," Alex said calmly.

"Not without an attorney, he's not!"

"Do you have one coming?" I asked.

"In this weather?" Gloria snapped. "Of course not! I barely made it here myself in one piece. No lawyer is coming, so I demand you let my son go!"

"Not happening," I said.

The front door opened, and Deputy Sparks stepped inside. His eyes quickly took in the scene, and he took a step behind Gloria, hands on his hips and ready to go.

"We have enough evidence to detain your son," Alex said. "If he has retained counsel, then we'll wait until the attorney gets here."

Gloria threw up a hand. "That's ridiculous! I just told you no one is coming in this weather!"

"Then Parker can stay here and stay safe," Alex said. "End of story."

"This isn't over," Gloria hissed. "Do you hear me?"

"Would you like me to escort you to your vehicle safely?" Grant asked. "I would be more than happy to do that."

"Stay away from me," Gloria snapped. "I'll find my own way out." She turned...and almost smacked into Deputy Sparks. "You people are everywhere!" She sidestepped him, opened the door, then slammed it shut.

"Well, I see the storm isn't the only excitement going on," Deputy Sparks deadpanned.

"I'm going to drive over to Across the Bridge Trinkets," I said. "I want to look around and see if I can find signs of an attempted break in. We know Linus died at home, but it could be Parker and Linus fought outside the store."

"That evidence probably washed away," Alex said.

I nodded. "Probably. But I just can't sit around here and do nothing."

"Why don't—" Alex's cell phone rang, cutting him off. "It's the emergency line." He ran his finger across the icon. "This is Sheriff Stone." He nodded, his eyes meeting Grant's. "We'll be right there."

"What is it?" Grant asked the minute Alex disconnected.

"Didn't we tell people not to go out in the storm unless it was an emergency?" Alex grumbled. "That was Gertrude Anise. She was out for a walk—why? I don't know!—and she saw two overturned trees on Celestial Way. One of the trees crushed a mailbox, a car, and is now blocking the road. Around the corner on Cauldron Street, she saw a submerged vehicle with someone inside, pounding on the windows and screaming. She said she thought it was Claudia Curseman."

"She's a normal," I said. "She's probably frantic."

"Grant and I will see to Claudia and the downed tree," Alex said. "Deputy Sparks, put Parker in the cell. If you get an emergency call, leave him there and go answer your call."

"Sure thing, Sheriff." Deputy Sparks gave me a nod, then strode toward the interview room.

I couldn't help but smile when I heard Parker's shrill voice a few seconds later. "Somebody help! Get it away! Those things are sharp!"

Alex rolled his eyes. "Why that porcupine feels the need to torture every suspect, I'll never understand."

I grinned. "Because he can."

Alex and Grant strode to the front door.

"Shayla," Grant said. "If you can, will you run by the bakery and make sure Serena is on her way home?"

"Of course."

As the door closed, Needles zipped out from the back of the station and barreled toward me, his wings glowing purple and green.

"I almost had him talking, Princess. Just five more minutes, and he'd have been squealing and telling all his secrets."

"Come on, we need to go check on Serena real quick at the bakery. Then, I want to drive out to Across the Bridge Trinkets and look around."

23

"That doesn't look good, Princess," Needles said from the backseat as I pulled to a stop behind Serena's car parked along the sidewalk.

Her head was on the steering wheel...and she was completely motionless. Heart pounding, I reached for the door handle, only to miss it in my haste. Telling myself to calm down, I unbuckled my seatbelt and reached for the door handle again.

This time I connected.

"Stay here," I said to Needles as I dropped to the street. "I'll be right back."

Serena must have heard me because she lifted her head off the steering wheel and looked over her right shoulder to the backseat. I could just make out the tops of the twins' car seats.

I knocked on her window, causing her to scream and whirl to face me. Laughing, she rolled down her manual window. "You scared me. I didn't see you come up. I guess I was too focused on the twins."

"Everything okay?"

Lightning lit up the sky, and Cayden and Brooke let out tiny screams of joy from the backseat. Serena laughed. "Hearing them laugh makes everything okay." Booming thunder quickly followed the lightning. "But, no. Everything isn't okay. My car won't start."

I snorted as I bent down to wave at the twins. "Of course it won't. It's like thirty years old. And before you point out my Bronco is older, it's a bad-ass Bronco, not a thirty-year-old Honda."

Serena's lips twitched. "Having an older car wasn't a big deal when I lived in town, but now that I'm out by you on the northeast side of the island, my car is racking up the mileage. I guess it's time to get a new one. Grant will be pleased. He's been begging me to trade for a year now."

"C'mon." I opened her door. "Help me get these precious babies into the Bronco."

"Are you heading home?"

"I was going to make a quick stop at Eldon's store, but I don't have to. It's more important we get you guys home safely."

"Thanks, Shayla." Serena wrenched open the backseat and unbuckled the car seats. Waving her hand through the air, she sent Cayden my way. Giggling and wiggling his fingers, he floated toward me. I grabbed hold of his car seat and hurried to the Bronco. I'd just gotten him buckled in when Serena opened the passenger-side door and leaned the seat forward to put Brooke in the back.

"Your old Bronco is not conducive to backseat riders," Serena laughed. "Just in case you needed to know."

I grinned. "I don't often have to haul around babies, so there's that."

Serena finished buckling in Brooke, backed out butt-first through the narrow opening, and then dropped down onto the sidewalk...just as the sky opened and the rain came down twice as hard and fast as it had been.

Screaming and laughing, Serena and I jumped inside the Bronco and slammed the doors shut...then looked at each other. We were soaked. Laughing some more, we turned to look at Needles and the twins in the back. Needles was sitting between the two car seats, wings glowing purple and green, and grinning like a loon. The twins were babbling and trying to hold hands.

"Let's go home." I started the Bronco and pulled slowly onto the road. There wasn't another car in sight, which was good. People were hopefully taking the hurricane warning seriously.

"What about stopping by Eldon's store?" Serena asked.

I shook my head. "We can do that tomorrow. We need to get home."

We rode in silence—listening to the rhythmic thumping of the windshield wipers on high—for about ten minutes while Serena texted Grant she and the twins were safe and headed home with me. She then texted GiGi, Aunt Starla, and Mom in our group chat, letting them know we were heading home. GiGi texted they were making good progress with trying to steer the eye away from the island, while Aunt Starla texted she and Walt were still in town checking on those who needed help.

We were almost to the turnoff that would lead to Eldon's store when my cell phone rang.

"It's Tommy." Serena picked up the phone off the console, slid her finger over the icon, and put it on speakerphone for me.

"Hey, Tommy," I yelled out to be heard over the pounding rain. "What's up?"

"Shayla! I'm glad the call finally went through. I've been trying to call for a couple minutes now. I'm on the road that leads to Eldon's store and to Pepper's place, and a tree is blocking the road. There's no way for vehicles to get in and out if there was an emergency situation. I'm a little worried. The tree is too big for me to move alone, but with some magic, it shouldn't be too hard."

My eyes met Serena's briefly before turning back to the road. I'd have to make a decision within the next twenty seconds or so. Stop and help...or get everyone in the Bronco home before the storm hit.

"We need to stop," Serena whispered. "You and I both know it's the right thing to do. How many houses are on that lane?"

"Five, I think."

"Shayla?" Tommy called. "Are you there?"

"I'm here!" I yelled. "We're actually just at the turnoff right now. It'll be about five minutes before we can reach you in this rain, though. Hold tight."

"Thank you! I'm nervous about Pepper and the kids being out there alone. Pepper said Devona left around 1:00, so she's been out there alone for the last two hours! I'd have come sooner had I known."

"Be there shortly, Tommy," Serena promised before disconnecting.

"Call the guys and let them know what we're doing," I said. "If the call can't go through, text them." I flashed her a grin. "I'm not taking the heat on this one for not getting you home in time."

Surprisingly, the call went through. When Serena explained what was going on, I expected to hear yelling from Alex and Grant...instead, they both were surprisingly calm.

"It might be best if you stayed at Pepper's cottage," Alex said. "Word on the east side is the eye should pass in about twenty minutes, and it'll go right through the east side. So staying where you are is the safest bet."

"What about you two?" I asked. "Where are you?"

"We just finished the last of our emergency calls," Grant

called out. "We're going back to the station to check on Parker Stonebridge and to take shelter at the station."

"We'll keep you updated," Serena promised before disconnecting.

I saw Tommy in the middle of the road up ahead and slowed down. The tree wasn't near as big as some I'd seen around town. Serena and I could move it using magic with no problem.

"He looks drenched," Needles said. *"I think I'll stay in the Bronco with the twins. Make sure they stay safe."*

"Big of you," I deadpanned.

Pulling to a stop next to Tommy's truck, I flipped up the hood on my raincoat and turned to Serena. "You might be able to stay inside the Bronco and just use your magic to help guide me."

"Not a chance," Serena said. "I'll get out and help. Needles can guard the babies."

As if on cue, the twins started to babble in their own language.

"Mommy and Auntie will be right back," Serena said. "You two be good for Needles."

We hopped out of the Bronco and took off running toward Tommy. He raised his hand in greeting.

"Thanks for coming!" he shouted over the pounding rain. "I was about to just take off and walk through the woods."

Through the driving rain, I could just make out Eldon's store up ahead on the left. I knew the lane went past the store and wound around to the left before dead-ending almost directly behind the shop.

"Let's get this tree moved!" I yelled. "Serena, why don't you take—"

I broke off when the tree levitated in front of our eyes. Startled, the three of us stumbled backward, unsure of what we were seeing.

"Is that you?" Tommy demanded.

I shook my head. "No!" Turning to Serena, I could tell from her wide-eyed look it wasn't her either. "Who is—"

All three of us turned as one toward the Bronco. Needles, wings glowing red, was up against the windshield, pounding frantically on the glass. Behind him, still buckled safely in their car seats, the twins were holding hands high in the air and babbling. At least, I assumed they were babbling…their mouths were moving. But then again, so was Needles'. Only I think he was silent screaming since I couldn't hear anything in my head.

The three of us took off sprinting for the Bronco, Serena leading the way, screaming and crying out for the twins. She'd just pulled open the passenger-side door when I yanked my driver's side door open, Tommy breathing heavy behind me.

"What are you two doing?" Serena demanded.

"Did you see that!" Needles shouted. *"Holy Sassafras, Princess! Did you see that?"*

Giggling loudly, connected hands still waving frantically in the air, the twins continued using magic to move the tree.

Serena and I popped back out of the Bronco, Tommy stepping back as well. Needles also zipped outside, no longer caring about the downpour. As if being pulled by a string, the four of us made our way to the front of the Bronco, staring at the most amazing sight ever. The tree was now levitated a good six feet in the air, directly over the hood of Tommy's truck. Slowly, the massive tree was being moved off the road…nice and slow.

Just when the trunk and roots were about to clear Tommy's truck, one end dropped down and landed with a crash. I winced when Tommy's hood crunched under the weight of the tree. High-pitched squeals and baby babble from inside the Bronco quickly righted the end of the tree trunk, and it once again moved slowly off the road.

"Sorry about that, Tommy," Serena said woodenly.

I laughed. "I can hear the panic in your voice, Serena."

Tommy waved her apology away with his hand. "I'm just glad I was here to see it! I can brag to people, 'I was there when…' and tell everyone what I just saw. Your twins are something, Serena." He turned back to look inside the Bronco. "I've been looking for some new bouncers down at the bar. I might be interested in hiring the twins!"

"Baby bouncers!" Needles cried, turning somersaults in the air, his wings glowing purple and green. *"We got us some baby bouncers!"*

24

Since Tommy's truck hood was smashed to smithereens, he grabbed the dinner still inside and hopped into the Bronco with us. If there was an emergency, a vehicle could still get around Tommy's truck without a problem.

Windshield wipers on high, I crept slowly past Across the Bridge Trinkets and farther down the lane. Curving to the left, I carefully avoided the pine branches sticking out in the road from the overgrown forest trees. With the extra tree coverage, though, the rain wasn't coming down near as hard and fast, so I turned the windshield wipers down.

I was almost at the cottage when my cell phone rang.

"I'll get it." Serena leaned forward from the backseat where she was snuggled tightly between the two car seats, snatched my phone off the console, and then put it on speakerphone. "Hey, Finn. It's Serena. I got you on speakerphone. How's the storm in town?"

"Still coming down, but according to the last update from

Doc's dragon friends in the sky, the eye of the storm will pass over the eastern side of the island in about five minutes."

"Thanks for the update." I pulled to a stop in Pepper's driveway and shut off the Bronco. "What's up?"

"I got the last of the broken pieces put together," she said. "Evidence is now ready to be cataloged. Thought you'd like to see the finished product. I'm going to send you a picture now."

I heard the notification ding. "Got it, Finn. Hold on, I'll pull it up."

Tommy reached for the handle. "I'm going to go on in, okay? Give Pepper the food I brought for dinner tonight."

I nodded absently, still staring at my phone. "Sure. We'll follow in a second."

"Tommy?" Finn's voice called out through the phone. "Is that you?"

Tommy laughed. "It's me. I got stranded, and the gang came to pick me up." He hopped out and grabbed the bag of food on the floorboard.

"I think I'll go with Tommy," Needles said. *"I'm starving."*

Serena laughed. "Tommy, Needles wants to go with you. Hold the door for him."

Needles zipped out the passenger-side door and hovered near Tommy's shoulder as he shut the door and turned to cross in front of the Bronco.

I frowned down at my phone. "Why are the wind chimes in the back separate from the other glass pieces?"

"They were all undamaged. They were on the floor, but not broken. I thought it odd as well when I was bagging, but I didn't think anything about it until I laid it all out. Does it mean something to you?"

"Not really—oh, my goddess! Why didn't I see this before?

Finn, I need to go." Disconnecting, I turned to Serena in the back. "I think I know who the killer is!"

A loud crash had me whirling to look out my driver's side window. The front window of the cottage had cracked, but not shattered. Tommy yelled and dropped the food. He was sprinting for the front door before I could even get my hand on the handle.

Then, just as quickly...Tommy came to an abrupt stop. It was obvious he was unable to move by the way his arms swung out around his body and his feet stayed planted on the ground.

"What's going on?" Serena shouted.

I opened my door and stepped out. "Stay here! Do *not* come anywhere near this cottage with those babies!" Shutting the door, I sprinted to where Tommy was howling like a madman, trying to move.

"It's magic of some kind, Princess," Needles said, his wings glowing red and blue. *"I just can't—"*

"I think I know," Serena said from behind us.

I whirled, heart pounding. "I told you to stay inside out of harm's way!" I instinctively reached out to grab one of the twins hovering in the air, rain pooling down her little baby rain slicker...but Brooke easily levitated away from me. "Why are they hovering?"

Serena giggled. "I can hear the panic in your voice, Shayla."

"It was funny when I said it to you," I muttered.

"Why can't I move?" Tommy demanded. "They need me inside."

It was true. I could make out shouting inside. Brooke babbled twice, then laid a tiny fist on Tommy's cheek. Like me, he instinctively reached out to grab her. But she wasn't having it. She moved back and chattered with Cayden.

"I think they were frightened for Tommy to run in there,"

Serena said. "They were fighting against the car seats. When I didn't move fast enough, they used their magic to stop him."

"I need in there!" Tommy shouted. "They need me!"

"Just wait a minute," I said, trying to maintain a sense of calm...even though I wasn't feeling it. I knew this was going to be disastrous no matter what happened.

I couldn't have the babies anywhere near this fight! Grant, Alex, Mom, Aunt Starla, GiGi, and everyone else would have my head on a platter if they knew Cayden and Brooke were within thirty yards of here.

"We need a plan," I whispered.

Brooke clapped her hands.

"A plan that doesn't include you two little werewitches," I added.

Cayden and Brooke both shrieked and babbled their displeasure.

"This is crazy," Tommy muttered.

"Let's stop and think," I said.

"I'll go down the chimney and see what I can find."

Needles zipped away to the top of the chimney.

"Who do you think is in there?" Serena asked.

Lightning flashed overhead, and the babies were momentarily entertained as they babbled and squealed. Forcing down my rising panic at the thought of them being outside the Bronco, I thought about what I knew.

"It's one of two people," I said, still trying to work through it.

"Why?" Tommy and Serena asked.

"Parker Stonebridge is sitting in a jail cell right now." I cut my eyes to Tommy. "Barton Longtree and his granddaughter, Ellie, would have no reason to hurt Pepper. I thought it might be Dalton because the wind chimes were untouched in the fight. I was thinking maybe he didn't want his stuff damaged. But I realize now that the undamaged wind chimes was out of respect."

"Who is it?" Tommy whispered. "Who's inside?"

"Vera Wingsom," I said.

"Princess!" Needles shouted over the wind. *"You aren't going to believe this!"*

25

I turned to Tommy. "Is there an entrance around back?"

"Yes. Goes into the kitchen."

I nodded. "Okay. Tommy, you go around back and enter that way. But stay out of the way until it's time to strike. Serena, you and the twins are staying out here or in the Bronco. Whatever. But you *aren't* going inside. Do you understand?"

Cayden and Brooke each instantly pitched a baby fit, but Serena nodded. "I understand. We'll stay out here."

"Needles, is it Vera Wingsom?" I asked.

"Yes. Vera has Jacob. And if this wasn't such a serious situation, I'd totally high-five Mia. She's running around the living room throwing magic at Vera and then running and hiding and laughing. I think that's how the glass got shattered."

I bit back a smile. Why was I not surprised by that news? "Tommy, go around back. Needles, hit the chimney. I'm going in the front way."

Serena grabbed Cayden and Brooke out of the air and planted them each on a hip. She crept over to the side of the house to get out of the rainstorm. Nodding once, I climbed the two steps and checked the door.

It was unlocked.

Pushing the door open, I stepped inside.

"That's far enough," Vera called out. "Unless you *want* me to hurt the boy. I've about had it with the little brat too! Whoever heard of a toddler wielding magic? It's unnatural!"

I bit back a laugh. Vera thought a toddler wielding magic was odd...try seeing babies doing it!

"It's all their fault we're in this situation as it is!" Vera screamed, pulling Jacob against her.

"How's that?" I mused, shutting the door behind me.

The cottage was one big great room. There was a hallway to my right, while the living room was to my left, and directly behind the living room was the kitchen. There were three barstools in front of the counter, and directly behind that was the back door where Tommy now stood, still outside and watching through the window.

Pepper Hollis was standing in front of the bar, her small, pale body shaking violently...her eyes never leaving her son's. Jacob was being held by the back of his shirt by Vera Wingsom, who was standing with her back against the far wall. And Mia was in the living room, looking calm and gleeful as she waved her chubby little arms at me from behind the recliner. Did she think this was a game? Is that why she seemed so unaffected by it all?

Needles flew out from the chimney and barreled straight for Mia, his wings glowing purple and green.

"Pretty!" Mia cried, reaching out to grab Needles.

He settled on the armchair of the recliner. *"I'll keep Mia distracted, Princess, while you and Tommy take out the fairy."*

"And I'll help."

I glanced over at the fireplace mantle and saw Ms. P perched high.

"I've been trying to make sure the little girl doesn't get hurt," Ms. P continued, *"but if the porcupine will watch her, then I can help you."* She reached out and unleashed her sharp claws. *"Just give me the sign."*

"Thank you, Ms. P," Needles said.

Unsure how to untangle the mess before me without Jacob and the others getting hurt, it took a moment for me to realize Vera was talking. I'd totally missed her confession.

"All he had to do was accept me," she was saying. "But, no! He could never do that! He couldn't see me for who I really was!"

Needles snorted. *"I think he totally saw her for what she totally was. Hence, no hookup with Vera."*

"Why kill Eldon?" I asked. "You loved him."

"I went out to the shop yesterday morning to ask Eldon to reconsider cutting Dalton's pay. I knew the boy was struggling to make ends meet. After I pled my case, he told me it didn't matter, anyway. He was dying, and to make sure his shop lived on, he went and sold it to Tommy Trollman." She narrowed her gaze at Pepper. "And then he went on to say that if Tommy was smart, he'd get Pepper to manage the place!" She raised a hand in the air. "That should have been my job! I should have been the one he turned to in his time of need! I was the one who'd loved him for over fifty years! Not you! Not some floozy wiggling her young hips at my man!" She barred her teeth, and I could feel magic crackling in the air. "You did this! It's all your fault! When Eldon said he hoped you'd run the shop, I saw red. I don't even remember picking up the cast iron cauldron and hitting him upside the head. But I must have because when I came to, he was on the ground bleeding out. I decided to make it look like a robbery, so I broke most of the items in the shop and even tried prying that stupid cabinet open. I then went out to my car to leave, and that's when I heard *her* inside the store!"

"And Linus Gallion?" I mused, stepping closer to Vera, purposely trying to get her to focus on me and not Pepper. "Why kill him? That's the one I can't figure out."

Vera sent a wave of magic my way, which I easily batted away.

"Stay back!" she screamed. "Or I swear, I'll kill everyone in this room! I have nothing to live for anymore!"

"Be careful, Princess!" Needles cried out.

"Why kill Linus Gallion?" I repeated.

"I drove out here last night to spy on her and the brats. Scare her a little. I saw Pepper's name on the jelly jar, so I know it was her who found Eldon. I wanted her to pay for taking away the love of my life!"

"He was never yours, Vera," I said.

"He was *always* mine." She shoved more magic at me, and this time I let it hit me, tuning out the whimper Jacob gave. I wanted Vera to feel like she was in control…before I took her down. "I left my car hidden behind some trees and walked through the woods. When it became obvious the troll in her front yard wasn't going anywhere, I sneaked back to my car and left. I was driving down the lane when I noticed two people trying to break into the store. I recognized the Stone boy immediately. That's when I got the brilliant idea to kill the other guy and frame Stone—you know, just in case you were looking hard at me or Dalton. I had one of Stone's zipper pulls in my car. The dumb kid had given it to me one day. Like I'd *actually* wear it. So I followed the other guy home. When I saw he lived in an apartment, I went with the odds he lived alone. I knocked on his door, and when he opened it, I used magic to subdue him. After killing him, I placed the zipper pull in his hand, hoping you guys would think he ripped it off Stone's shirt."

"And now here we are," I said. "You standing in an innocent woman's home, scaring her and her children, all because your little ego can't deal with the fact a man you loved didn't love you back."

"Witch!" Vera screamed, pushing Jacob aside and rounding on me. "You'll pay for that!"

"Bring it," I said, motioning for Pepper to grab Jacob.

Out of my periphery, I saw Ms. P leap down from the fireplace mantle. I was about to grab my Binder when Vera hissed and turned around to face Pepper and Jacob. Magic flew from Vera's hands, and since Pepper was using her arms to protect her son, Pepper took the hit fully in her chest. It rocked her backward, and Pepper and Jacob fell to the ground.

"No!" Tommy shouted as he kicked open the back door and charged inside.

Wild now, Vera turned on Tommy and was about to unleash another round of magic, when Ms. P jumped on Vera's back. Not wanting to throw the Binder and cage Ms. P in with Vera, I clipped the Binder back on my belt and waited until Vera turned around to face me. She was screaming and trying to dislodge the cat. The minute Vera turned to me, I tackled her legs and brought her down on top of me. Flipping her over, I wrestled her hands behind her back so she couldn't hit me with her magic.

"Excellent job, Princess!" Needles cried from the living room.

Claws still out, Ms. P walked down Vera's back and rested on her butt...painfully kneading the plump mounds with her razor-like nails. Tuning out Vera's screams of pain, I glanced over at Pepper. Tommy had Pepper and Jacob in his arms, making sure they were okay.

"Up! Up!" Mia screamed, racing from behind the recliner to Tommy. "Me, up!"

Laughing, Tommy bent down and scooped the precocious little girl into his arms. "You did good, Miss Mia."

"Everyone okay in here?" Serena asked from the doorway.

I looked over at her and grinned. The twins were babbling and squirming against Serena's hips, obviously not happy with being left out of everything going on. "We're good, thanks. Ms. P, if you're done getting your licks in, I'd like to properly subdue Vera, please."

Ms. P gave one more swipe at Vera's backside before jumping off. Pushing off her myself, I whipped out my Binder and encased Vera in the magical bubble that would strip her of her witch magic.

"I already called Alex and Grant," Serena said. "They should be here shortly."

"Thank you," Pepper choked out, hugging her children to her. "Thank you all." She looked up at Tommy and gave a watery laugh. "I'm not sure how I'm going to explain to my new landlord how the door got broken."

Tommy threw back his head and laughed. "I wouldn't worry about him. I hear he's a pretty forgiving guy. Got a big heart too. Just ask the sheriff when he gets here." He winked at her. "He'll vouch for me."

I laughed. "You wish!"

26

"*It is not often I am rendered speechless, Daughter of my Heart,*" Dad said.

The eye of the storm had long past, and now we were just getting the tail end of the rains. By the time Vera Wingsom was hauled down to the station, Parker released, and PADA called for a pickup...it was almost eight o'clock.

Grant, obviously dazed by the twins' powerful abilities when Tommy told the story of how his truck got smashed, had taken Serena and the babies straight home from Pepper's cottage. At this rate, the poor werewolf was going to go gray before the twins got out of puberty.

"I'm still kicking myself for not putting the wind chime clue together sooner," I said to Dad.

"*You can't blame yourself for that, Princess,*" Needles said, floating down from Dad's branches to land on my shoulder.

"*Needles is correct,*" Dad said. "*From what you have told me, most of the clues pointed in a different direction.*"

"I know." Sighing, I settled back against Dad's trunk. "The east side of the island held up pretty good."

Dad chuckled. *"It did. I have to tell you, I have not felt such a powerful storm in many years."*

"Alex and Deputy Sparks are still patrolling the east side, marking places we'll need to meet tomorrow to clean up."

"Have you spoken to Tommy tonight?" Dad asked.

"Oh, yeah. After we left Pepper's cottage to go to the station, he called Weston to come tow his truck, and then he called his handyman to come fix the door. He said the kids are doing great." I laughed. "He'd brought in the food from outside, and it was still good. Jacob was excited to eat something other than chicken strips, and Mia was still chattering about playing hide and seek and chase." I shook my head. "I guess a part of me is thankful she is too young to understand just how serious things were."

"But Ms. P was the one who saved the day," Needles said.

Again, I laughed. "Yeah, she really was. And I think she'll learn to really love her new home." I turned to face Dad. "But that's not the biggest thing Tommy told me. Tommy and Pepper both heard from Eldon's attorney. He informed Pepper that Eldon's will left her all the money in his savings account, *and* she also inherited his rare, expensive vintage collection."

"That is wonderful news," Dad said. *"Now Pepper can really start over."*

I nodded. "Yes, without having to feel like she's indebted to Eldon and Tommy. She finally has something of her own."

"And with Devona Flame befriending Pepper," Dad said, *"that should help as well."*

"Speaking of." I rested back against Dad's trunk once again. "Only one more week until their big day, *and* Tamara adopts Jayden. Good news all around."

"And the island could use this good news," Needles said.

"That's the truth." I stood and stretched. "I better get back home. Zoie is going to call me around 9:00 tonight. She texted me earlier and said she needed to do some girl talking. So I want to make sure my phone is fully charged." I grinned. "I never know when Zoie calls how long it'll be for."

"Tell Young Zoie I cannot wait until she graduates and returns home to the island," Dad said.

"Will do." I reached out and wrapped my arms around Dad's trunk, pressing my cheek against his rough bark. "Love you, Dad."

"And I love you, Daughter of my Heart."

* * *

Are you ready for the next book in the series? Then click here and get *Deadly Tempo*. Tamara and Zac are getting married…if only the wedding vendors would stop dropping dead! Deadly Tempo

* * *

Love the idea of a Valkyrie witch teaming up with a Fallen Angel to solve crimes? Then the paranormal cozy series, A Kara Hilder Mystery, should be right up your alley! A spinoff from the A Witch in the Woods, this crime-solving duo not only works for their supernatural town of Mystic Cove, but they also work for the Paranormal Apprehension and Detention Agency—which means they travel undercover to take down bad guys. Click here to read Book 1, *Sounds of Murder*: Sounds of Murder

What happens when a mermaid-witch detective teams up

with a treasure-hunting demigod with a snarky miniature glow-in-the-dark dragon named Glo? Find out in this humorous paranormal cozy series that is yet another spin-off from the A Witch in the Woods. Click here and get book 1, *Tangled Waters,* from the Enchanted Waters Mystery series: Tangled Waters

Do you love the idea of a time-traveling, cold-case solving witch? Then Lexi and her side-kick detective familiar, Rex the Rat, are just what you're looking for! Check out their first stop to 1988 in *Time After Time* Time After Time

Have you read the hilarious adventures of Ryli Sinclair and Aunt Shirley? This traditional cozy mystery series is always fast-paced and laugh-out-loud funny. But what else would you expect from Aunt Shirley—a woman who has at least two deadly weapons on her at all times and carries her tequila in a flask shoved down her shirt? Book 1 is *Picture Perfect Murder*! Picture Perfect Murder

Love the idea of a bookstore/bar set in the picturesque wine country of Sonoma County? Then join Jaycee, Jax, Gramps, Tillie, and the whole gang in this traditional cozy series as they solve murders while slinging suds and chasing bad guys in this family-oriented series. First book is *Murder on the Vine!* Murder on the Vine

Or maybe you're in the mood for a romantic comedy…heavy on comedy and light on sweet romance? Then the Trinity Falls series is for you! Trouble in Trinity Falls

Looking for a paranormal cozy series about a midlife witch looking to make a new start with a new career? Then A Witch in the Woods is the book series for you! A game warden witch, a talking/flying porcupine, and a gargoyle sheriff! Check out Book 1, *Deadly Claws,* in this prolific series that has caused myriad spinoffs: Deadly Claws

ABOUT THE AUTHOR

Jenna writes paranormal and contemporary cozies. Her humorous characters and stories revolve around over-the-top family members and creative murders. Jenna currently lives in Missouri with her husband, stepdaughter, mother, Nova Scotia duck tolling retriever dog, Brownie, and her tuxedo-cat, Whiskey.

When she's not writing, Jenna likes to attend beer and wine tastings, go antiquing, visit craft festivals, and spend time with her family and friends. Check out her website at http://www.jennastjames.com/. When you sign up for her newsletter, you'll not only receive a free box set, but you'll also be able to keep up with the latest releases! Other important links:

Author Page: facebook.com/jennastjamesauthor

Jenna's Reading Crew Facebook Page: https://www.facebook.com/groups/2787636591248452

Bookbub: https://www.bookbub.com/profile/jenna-st-james

Made in the USA
Coppell, TX
06 August 2024

35682082R00089